Main Street
Needle and Thread

Also by Ann M. Martin

Main Street series
Welcome to Camden Falls

The Babysitters Club series
The Summer Before
Kristy's Great Idea
Claudia and the Phantom Phone Calls
The Truth About Stacey
Mary Anne Saves the Day
Dawn and the Impossible Three

Main Street
Needle and Thread

ANN M. MARTIN

SCHOLASTIC

Scholastic Children's Books
A division of Scholastic Ltd
Euston House, 24 Eversholt Street
London, NW1 1DB, UK
Registered office: Westfield Road, Southam, Warwickshire, CV47 0RA
SCHOLASTIC and associated logos are trademarks and/or
registered trademarks of Scholastic Inc.

First published in the United States of America by Scholastic Inc., 2007
This edition published in the UK by Scholastic Ltd, 2012

Text copyright © Ann M. Martin, 2007
The right of Ann M. Martin to be identified
as the author of this work has been asserted by her.

ISBN 978 1407 12484 1

A CIP catalogue record for this book
is available from the British Library

Printed and bound by CPI Group (UK) Ltd, Croydon, CR0 4YY
Papers used by Scholastic Children's Books are made
from wood grown in sustainable forests.

13 5 7 9 10 8 6 4 2

www.scholastic.co uk/zone

This book is for Emma Kosi

Autumn in Camden Falls

On a September day, the last day of summer vacation for the children of Camden Falls, Massachusetts, a chilly breeze blew through town.

"Good gravy, it's cool this morning!" Min Read exclaimed to her granddaughters as they stepped outside. "I think I need to grab a sweater. Are you two going to be warm enough?"

"Yup," Flora and Ruby answered.

And Ruby added, "We don't need sweaters."

As Min hurried back inside, the girls danced through the carpet of acorns on the pavement in front of the Row Houses, where they lived with their grandmother.

"Are you nervous about tomorrow?" Flora asked her sister.

"About starting school?"

Flora nodded.

"A little," admitted Ruby. She would be starting fourth grade and Flora would be starting sixth. "But I'm not going to think about that. I'm trying to memorize all the songs from *Annie*. That's my goal."

"Your goal for what?" asked Flora.

"Just my goal. In case I'm ever asked to audition for a production of the show. It could happen, you know." Then, seeing the expression on Flora's face, she added hurriedly, "Well, it *could*."

"I didn't say it couldn't."

"You were thinking it."

"How do you know what I was thinking?"

"Girls?" said their grandmother as she emerged from their house wearing a sweater she had knitted herself. "Do I hear squabbling?"

"No," said Flora as she set off down the pavement.

"Yes," said Ruby. "But not bad squabbling." She kicked an acorn ahead of her as she ran after her grandmother and sister. For an old lady, Min was pretty quick. And busy, which was why, when Flora and Ruby were much smaller, they had begun to call her Min. It was short for Mindy, which was her name, and for "In a minute", which she used to say all the time.

Ruby skipped along. *"Send a flood, send the flu, anything that you can dooooo,"* she sang, and she let her voice rise, *"to little giiiiirls!"*

Ahead of her, Min turned around. "What on earth is she singing?" she asked Flora.

"It's OK. It's a song from *Annie*."

"Lord love a duck," murmured Min.

Flora retreated into silence. She was cataloguing the signs of fall that they passed on their way to Needle and Thread, the sewing store that Min owned with her friend Mrs Walter. Above, the dry leaves in the oak trees rattled in the breeze. In the garden of a house on the other side of Aiken Avenue, one entire flower bed was now overrun with lavender autumn crocuses, their long leaves spilling over the rocky border and on to the lawn. On some of the fir trees, Flora could see tiny pine cones. She thought of collecting a basketful of them and painting them gold and silver to use in Christmas decorations.

And with that one simple thought, which last year would have brought her such pleasure, a curtain fell across Flora's brain. She drew in several deep breaths as she trotted along with Min.

Min glanced at her. "Everything all right, honey?"

"Yup," said Flora. She loved Min, but she found

3

herself unable to share her new worries with her. She willed herself to chase away the thoughts in her head and tried concentrating on the sounds behind her.

". . . betcha they're smart. Bet they collect things like ashtrays and aaaaart!"

Flora thought about the photo in her pocket, the one that had so frightened her the night before. She put her hand on it to make sure it was there. She planned to show it to her friend Olivia later that morning.

"Hurry up, girls!" Min called as she turned on to Main Street. "We're late this morning, and it's all my fault."

Moments later, Min Read and her granddaughters reached Needle and Thread. Flora flung open the door, the bell jangling above her. Mrs Walter, Olivia's grandmother (called Gigi by her grandchildren and by Flora and Ruby), had already put the coffee on and was arranging new sewing and quilting magazines in the rack near the cash register.

"I'm sorry we're late," said Min breathlessly. "I had to go back for a sweater."

"No worries," replied Mrs Walter. "I've only been here a few minutes myself."

During the next hour, Flora and Ruby helped Min

and Gigi get ready for the day, and then Flora plopped herself down on one of the couches at the front of Needle and Thread, the couches where customers sat when they dropped by for a chat-and-stitch. She gazed out of the wide window and watched Main Street come to life.

Flora and Ruby had lived in Camden Falls for just over two months, so watching Main Street come to life was still interesting, at least to Flora. She wondered if it would always be interesting. Or would she one day be so used to this town that she wouldn't notice the details any more? She thought about her old home, the town in which she and Ruby had grown up. She didn't remember many of the details. Was that because she had been so used to everything?

Flora stared moodily out of the window at Stuff 'n' Nonsense across the street. Maybe she should have paid more attention to her old town, to her street, her house, her room, her parents. But how could she have known it would all be taken away from her? She was thankful, of course, that after her parents' accident Min had been able to care for her and Ruby. And Flora liked Camden Falls. She did. She was making friends. There was Nikki, who'd recently started visiting Needle and Thread. And, of course, Olivia, who lived next door in the Row

Houses. Although Olivia was a year younger than Flora, she had skipped second grade and would be in Mrs Mandel's sixth-grade class with Flora and Nikki when school started the next day.

Flora liked Needle and Thread, too. She liked her other neighbours in the Row Houses. She liked lots of things here. But here wasn't home for Flora. Not yet.

Now autumn was arriving. Ordinarily, this was Flora's favourite time of the year. Ruby's, too. Autumn meant pumpkins and new shoes and a fresh school year. And it meant that the holidays were on the way. Halloween first, then Thanksgiving and Christmas. This was what made the curtain fall across Flora's brain: the holidays. How could she face them without her parents? How could Ruby and Min face them?

"Flora?" Flora felt her grandmother's hands on her shoulders and turned to see Min standing behind the couch. "It's your last day of vacation. Do you really want to sit here all morning? Soon enough you'll be complaining that you don't have any time for sewing or knitting or making cards."

Flora heaved a great sigh. "I know," she replied. She stood up wearily and looked around Needle and Thread. "Where's Ruby?"

"Running errands for Gigi and me."

Flora thought about strolling up and down Main Street until she found her sister. One of the best things about living in Camden Falls was being allowed freedom and independence. Her old home had been three kilometres from town – a town that was much bigger than Camden Falls. Flora and Ruby had never ever been allowed to roam it by themselves. But this new town was different. Main Street really was the main street, even though it was only a few blocks long. A person could walk from one end of downtown Camden Falls to the other in fifteen minutes. The Row Houses were a seven-minute walk, exactly, from Needle and Thread.

While Flora stood by the couch, deciding whether to find Ruby or to work on the patchwork quilt she had begun the week before, the bell over the door to the store jangled, and in walked Robby Edwards and his mother.

"Flora!" exclaimed Robby. "Good morning! We start school tomorrow. Are you excited? Are you scared?"

Flora smiled. "Hi, Robby," she said. Robby was seventeen years old and one of the most cheerful people Flora had ever met.

"I'm going to be in the high school," Robby went on.

Flora knew that Robby, who had Down syndrome, attended a special education class at Camden Falls Central High School.

"I'll be at Camden Falls Elementary," Flora said. "In sixth grade. Olivia and Nikki are going to be in my class. Ruby will be in fourth grade."

"I have Mrs Fulton," said Robby. "I always have her. She's very nice. She has lots of glue."

Robby left Flora and began wandering around Needle and Thread. He let his hand graze bolts of fabric as he passed the racks of quilting cottons. He examined the displays of buttons and laces. He eyed with interest the small table near the back of the store where old Mary Woolsey sat when she took in mending. He passed his mother, who was leafing through pattern books. Finally, he returned to the front of the store and looked at the flyers by the register.

"'Make a teddy bear'," he read aloud. "'Learn to sew, have fun, and help a kid in need.' Flora," he said, "what is this?"

"It's a class we're going to have here at the store," she explained.

"And it was all Flora's idea," a voice said. Flora

turned around to see Olivia come jangling through the door. "Hi, everyone!" Olivia called. "Hi, Gigi. Hi, Min. Hi, Robby."

"Hello, Olivia," replied Robby.

Olivia peered at the flyer Robby was holding. "These came out really well," she said.

"Camden Falls Art Supply printed them," said Gigi. "I picked them up on my way to the store this morning. They *did* come out well, didn't they?"

"But what do you mean, 'Learn to sew and help a kid in need'?" asked Robby.

"It's a really cool idea," said Olivia. "You can take the class for free. You sign up ahead of time, and when you come to the store, we give you everything you need to make a teddy bear. We'll help you make it – if you don't already know how to sew – and then all the finished bears will be donated to kids who . . ." (Olivia paused and glanced at Flora) "to kids who really need them."

"That's OK," said Flora. "You can say it. Robby, after the car accident—"

"The one you and Ruby were in with your parents?"

"Yes. After the car accident, when the police officer came to tell Ruby and me that our parents had died, she gave each of us a teddy bear. And then I read

organization that gives teddies to
need them – kids who are in the hospital,
have lost their homes, or who are really sad."

"ke you and Ruby," said Robby.

Flora swallowed. "Well, yes." Talking about the accident had become a little easier, but not much.

"I want to make a teddy bear," said Robby.

"Great. You can be the first one to sign up for a class," said Olivia.

Robby grinned and shouted across the store, "Mom, I'm going to learn to sew, have fun, and help a kid in need!"

The bell over the door jangled again . . . and again and again as customers came and went.

"Land sakes, what a busy morning," said Min.

Ruby returned from her errands, and she and Flora began assembling teddy bear kits for the classes. Olivia, who got paid to work at the store since her father had lost his job, rang up purchases while Min and Gigi helped customers. Olivia took her work very seriously.

It wasn't until after lunch that things quieted down, and when they did, Nikki arrived. She stepped cautiously through the door, barely causing the bell to ring.

"Hi," she said shyly.

"Nikki, dear," said Gigi. "How nice that you could stop by."

Nikki Sherman, scrawny and unkempt, lived on the outskirts of Camden Falls. Until her brother had found a bicycle at the dump and fixed it up for her, she hadn't had a way to come into town on her own. And she had even fewer reasons to do so. She almost never had money to spend, and until recently she'd had no friends, either. But the summer – and Flora and Ruby's arrival – had changed that.

Olivia, Ruby, Flora and Nikki sprawled on the couches at the front of Needle and Thread. Min and Gigi sat behind the counter while a sole customer roamed the store.

"I can't believe summer's over," said Olivia, letting out a loud sigh. "It always goes by too fast."

"I thought you liked school," said Ruby.

"I do. But I like vacation just as much."

"This summer seemed really long to me," said Flora.

"Me, too," said Nikki. "But I still don't want to go back to school."

"Why not?" asked Ruby. "School's fun. You get to be with your friends."

"*You* don't *have* friends yet," Flora said to Ruby. "I mean, friends your own age."

I do, too. Lacey is my age. Almost. And I'll have more friends soon. Nikki, how come you don't want to go to school?"

Nikki shrugged. "I just don't."

"Not even if you and Flora and I will be in the same class?" asked Olivia, who knew why Nikki didn't want to go to school. It must have been awful to be a Sherman in Camden Falls. The Shermans had an unfortunate reputation, mainly because Mr and Mrs Sherman drank too much and Mr Sherman had a terrible temper. The three Sherman kids showed up at school in ill-fitting clothes and were able to bathe only when the plumbing in their little house was in working order. Olivia hoped school might improve for Nikki now that they were all friends.

"Well, that will make it better," Nikki agreed. "Plus, we'll have Mrs Mandel."

Every student at Camden Falls Elementary hoped to get Mrs Mandel for sixth grade.

The girls lounged on the couches until Nikki looked at the Needle and Thread clock.

"Oh!" she cried. "I have to go! I promised Tobias I'd get home by three to take care of Mae so he can go to work. He got a part-time job at John's."

"John's?" said Flora.

"That auto body place out by the new grocery

store." Nikki jumped to her feet. "OK. I'll see you guys at school tomorrow. Wish me luck on the bus."

"Good luck," said Flora and Ruby dutifully.

And Olivia said, "Stick with Mae. Maybe no one will bother you if you're sitting with a first-grader."

The door closed behind Nikki, and Flora felt in her pocket for the photograph. Then she glanced at her sister. "Hey, Ruby. If you'll go to Ma Grand-mère to get chocolate chip cookies for you and Olivia and me, I'll pay for the cookies."

"Cool," said Ruby, who grabbed the money from her sister and was out the door before Flora could change her mind.

Flora scooted down the couch to Olivia and thrust the photo in front of her. "Look. Look at this," she said.

"What is it?" Olivia squinted at the picture of a young woman posing stiffly with a little girl.

"I found it in this box of papers that was in the attic," Flora replied. "I haven't told anyone about the box yet," she added, squirming slightly. "It's old family stuff and I kind of want to keep it a secret."

"Min's stuff? How come you want to keep it a secret?"

"I just do."

"OK. . . Who are these people?"

"That's just the thing. I've been looking at the picture over and over, thinking the woman is familiar. The little girl is my mother when she was four years old. See?" Flora turned over the photo to show Olivia the writing on the back. "It says 'Frannie and Mary – nineteen seventy.' Frannie is my mother. And at first I thought Mary might be Min's sister, Mary Elizabeth. A nice photo of my mother with her aunt. But take a look at the necklace Mary is wearing."

Olivia brought the photo closer to her face and gazed at it for a moment. Then she screamed and dropped the picture to the floor.

"*Shh!*" hissed Flora. She grabbed for the photo and turned around to look at Min and Gigi, but they were busy talking with the UPS woman who had arrived at the back door with a delivery. Then she clasped Olivia's hand. "It's who I think it is, isn't it?" she said quietly.

"Scary Mary," whispered Olivia, "wearing her star necklace."

"What was my mother doing with Mary Woolsey? I didn't think Mary knew my family back then."

"I have no idea," Olivia croaked, and she cleared her throat.

"Really? You don't have any idea at all? You've told me everything you know about Mary?"

"Cross my heart. She's, like, eighty years old. She lives alone – you saw her house. She's possibly a witch and definitely crazy. She's buried some kind of treasure in her garden and she keeps a child hidden in her basement."

Flora narrowed her eyes at Olivia.

"OK, those are just rumours. But they might be true."

"What else?"

"She catches rats in her attic and fries them up for dinner?" suggested Olivia.

"Come on. Tell me something that will help."

"I don't know anything more. I mean, anything more than you do. She comes here three times a week to take in people's mending and stuff, and to return it to them when it's finished. She's been doing that ever since the store opened, I think, and that's how she earns her money, thanks to Gigi and Min." Olivia looked at the photo again and shuddered. "I really don't know what she would have been doing with your mother." She paused. "Maybe your mother had a secret past."

Flora was about to reply when Ruby entered the store, holding aloft a paper bag from Ma Grand-mère. Flora stuffed the picture back in her pocket and whispered to Olivia, "We can discuss this later."

Now she had even more questions . . . and no answers. Although she did like the idea of someone, anyone, having a secret past.

2

A Peek in the Windows

If you had never before visited Camden Falls, you might first choose to walk down Main Street; you might walk from one end to the other, passing Frank's Beans and the used bookstore and the post office and Ma Grand-mère. You might pause to look in the window of Camden Falls Art Supply with its back-to-school theme, and the window of Needle and Thread, where Evelyn Walter and Min Read have already displayed orange and black Halloween fabrics. You might call hello to cranky Gina Grindle as she closes up Stuff 'n' Nonsense for the evening, and then you might glance curiously at Sonny Sutphin as he inches his wheelchair along the sidewalk. You might breathe in the aroma of oregano and cheese and tomato sauce as you pass College Pizza, and of chocolate and almonds and butterscotch as you pass Dutch Haus, the ice cream parlour.

At Dutch Haus, you would find yourself at one end of downtown Camden Falls, and you might choose to turn left off Main Street, and then right on to Aiken Avenue. If you did this, you would soon face a row of eight attached homes, a mansionlike block of granite known locally as the Row Houses. These homes, nearly identical to one another, once grand, now solidly practical, were built a hundred and twenty-five years before Flora and Ruby came to Camden Falls to live with their grandmother, which was seventy-one years after Min Read (then Mindy Davis) was born in the very house in which she now lives with Ruby and Flora.

If you were standing on Aiken Avenue not too long after Flora Northrop showed her friend Olivia Walter the mysterious photograph, you would be able to peek into the lives of the Row House residents on an early September evening, the night before school starts in Camden Falls.

In the house at the left end of the row, you would find the Morrises. There are four Morris children, and tomorrow Alyssa, the youngest, will begin all-day preschool, which means that for the first time, every Morris child will be in school five full days a week. Mrs Morris thought Alyssa would be thrilled to go off to school like her older sister and brothers, but now Alyssa is close to having a tantrum.

"I don't *want* to go to school," she cries, "and you can't make me."

"But, Lissy, school is fun," says Lacey, her big sister. "Especially preschool. You get to paint and make things and play games."

"I can do all those things with you and Travis and Mathias," says Alyssa, and her sister sighs in a very frustrated fashion.

Next door, old Mr Willet is just as frustrated as Lacey Morris, except that he's frustrated with his wife, who has been insisting all day that people are spying on her from inside their television set. She has draped the set with a towel, and anytime Mr Willet tries to fold it up and put it away, she exclaims, "But now they can see us! And I don't want people spying on me. I'm still in my nightie." This is not true. Mrs Willet is dressed. She has been dressed in the same outfit for three days straight. Mr Willet, for the life of him, can't convince her to take off the trousers and top he chose for her on Sunday morning. This business of dressing and undressing has been a problem all summer long, and he has no idea what to do about it. He has no idea what to do about the TV people, either.

In the house between the Willets' and the one Flora, Ruby and Min now share, you would find the Malones – Dr Malone, Camden Falls's dentist, and his daughters, Margaret and Lydia. Margaret is sixteen and will be a junior at Camden Falls Central High School. She is beginning to think about colleges and wishes her mother were alive to help her with the big decision she will soon have to make. Not that her father won't be helpful, but Margaret is thinking about going to Mount Holyoke, which is where her mother went to college.

Margaret's sister, Lydia, is fourteen and will be a freshman at Central. She has had a difficult summer and now, as she sits in her bedroom, she feels a wave of panic wash over her. Will she be able to avoid Brandi and the other kids who helped get her into trouble? It seems that this will be impossible once they are all in school together. Lydia throws herself on to her bed, iPod cranked up to full volume.

On the other side of the north wall of Lydia's bedroom, Flora Marie Northrop is at her desk. Spread around her are scraps of paper, several lace remnants, sequins, stamp pads in three different colours, and all of her birthday-themed rubber stamps. Flora is trying to concentrate on making a card for Olivia, whose birthday is coming up, but her mind keeps wandering to the next morning, when she will go to a brand-new school. She can't keep her heart from pounding in her ears.

The Walters live in the fifth Row House from the left, and on this evening, Olivia and her brothers and parents are having a family meeting. Olivia is growing more and more concerned about the fact that her father hasn't yet found another job. "Why don't *you* work, Mom?" she asks. "You could get a job."

"I may do that, Olivia," her mother replies. "There are all sorts of possibilities for your father and me. But we want you kids to understand that we will be OK for a while if neither of us is working. Truly. We're very lucky that we can afford to do that. We want to wait until just the right opportunity comes along. We may have to pinch pennies for a while, but we're going to be fine. OK?"

"OK," say Olivia and Henry and Jack.

Mr Pennington lives next door to Olivia's family, and on this warm evening, you wouldn't be able to see him from the street. He is sitting in a lawn chair in his back garden. The porch light is on, his old dog, Jacques, is at his feet, and he is gazing at the stars, thinking of nothing but how fine the night is and how he can't imagine anywhere else he would rather be at this particular moment. The only thing he might wish for would be his wife at his side. She would have enjoyed this evening, too.

Robby Edwards, one house over, is in the kitchen, bouncing enthusiastically up and down on his toes. "Tomorrow will be the first day of my last year of school," he says. "And then I am going to find a job. I want a job. I want to work. I want to work at Stuff 'n' Nonsense with all the fragile items."

His parents smile at him. "That certainly is one possibility," says his mother.

"But after you graduate, you could continue in school for four more years," his father reminds him. "There's a special programme at Central."

"Nope! Not for me! I want to work," says Robby, and his parents say, "We'll see."

In the very last of the Row Houses, Barbara and Marcus Fong sit together in their living room. They are leaning close to each other and reading the newspaper. Barbara looks up from her article, glances at her husband, pats her round belly, and says, "School starts tomorrow. Just think – six years from now we'll be getting ready to send our own child off to kindergarten."

"Maybe we'll have twins," says her husband. "Maybe we'll be getting two children ready."

"We'll know soon enough," says Barbara.

Now, having come to the end of the Row Houses, if you were to look to the evening sky as Mr Pennington is doing, you might find the Little Dipper. And if you were to lock your gaze on it, you and the constellation and Nikki Sherman would form a silent triangle, since several kilometres away Nikki, sitting in her darkened room, has turned her own face to the sky. It is too early for her to go to bed, even on a school night, but her little sister, Mae, with whom she shares the room, has fallen asleep, and Nikki doesn't dare leave this pocket of safety. Downstairs in the kitchen, her parents are having another fight. Words and plates fly through the air, and Nikki knows better than to call any attention to herself. She squeezes her eyes tightly shut and starts to recite "Twinkle, twinkle, little star" but stops before she reaches the end. She can never choose just one thing to wish for, so she makes no wish at all.

3

Mrs Mandel

The next morning, the Row House adults – every single one of them – stood on their front steps and called goodbye to the Row House kids. Even the Fongs and the Willets and Mr Pennington were there. They all waved to Margaret and Lydia as the doors to the Central High bus swooshed shut behind them and the girls lurched towards seats at the back. They called, "Have a good day, Robby!" as he stepped into the minivan that would transport him to Mrs Fulton's class. Robby flopped on to the front seat of the van and waved exuberantly out of the window. "I'll see you this afternoon!" he called back. Then the adults turned to the eight children who had gathered on the pavement in front of Min's house: Lacey, Travis and Mathias Morris; Olivia, Henry and Jack Walter; and Flora and Ruby Northrop.

"Have fun!" said Mr Fong.

"Come visit me after school and tell me what you're going to be reading this year," called Mr Pennington. "I always like to know." Mr Pennington had been both a teacher and a principal.

"Remember to come to the store this afternoon before you go anywhere else," Min said to Flora and Ruby.

"OK, OK," replied the girls, and Lacey added, "Alyssa, this afternoon you can tell us all about your school."

Then the Row House kids hurried along the pavement. When they came to the first corner, they turned right. All summer long, Flora and Ruby had turned left at this corner to accompany Min to Needle and Thread. Now they were turning right, and their next adventure was beginning. Flora glanced at her sister and found that Ruby was humming something under her breath and smiling.

"Are you ready?" asked Flora.

"Ready!" said Ruby.

"Who's your teacher this year?" Lacey asked Ruby, skipping ahead so she could walk next to her.

"Mr Lundy. In my old school, I would probably have had Mrs Erickson, and no one liked her. She never laughed. No one ever even saw her smile. She never took kids on field trips or let them do special projects like make volcanoes or learn to crochet. She was B-O-R-I-N-G. And a little mean."

"Not Mr Lundy," said Lacey. "He's supposed to be nice."

"You guys are going to like our school," said Olivia confidently. "It's really cool. We have an auditorium with a stage and real seats like in a theatre. And a gym and a cafeteria and a big library."

"And one whole room just for art," spoke up Jack, who was starting first grade and was very excited about joining the ranks of the big kids who went to the big school.

"And if you want to learn to play an instrument, you can take band after school," added Mathias, Lacey's twin. The twins would be in third grade.

"What's the principal like?" asked Ruby.

Flora giggled. "Ruby got to know our last principal pretty well. Didn't you, Ruby?"

"Those things were *not* my fault!"

Henry looked impressed. "What'd you do?"

Ruby ignored him. "Olivia," she said, "you're going to be ten on your birthday, instead of eleven like Flora, right?"

"The big one-oh," said Olivia.

"Really, Ruby, what did you do?" Henry, who was eight, asked again.

This time Ruby was saved by Travis. "Look – there it is!" he cried, pointing. "There's our school."

The children had reached an intersection that was busier than the others on their route. A man wearing a bright orange vest and holding up an equally bright orange sign stood on the corner.

"Hi, Charlie!" called Travis.

"Hi there, Travis," replied Charlie. "Welcome back."

"That's our lollipop man," Travis said to Flora and Ruby. "His real name is Charles, but he lets us call him Charlie."

The Row House kids stood in a pack behind Charlie. As he shepherded them across the street, Olivia said, "Charlie, these are our new friends, Flora and Ruby. They live next door to me."

"Greetings, Flora and Ruby," said Charlie. "I'm here to help you. If you ever run into trouble on your way to or from school, just come looking for me." Up close, Flora could see that Charlie's sparse hair was arranged in what her father would have called a "comb-over", but she didn't mind. Charlie had kind eyes.

27

On the other side of the street, Flora paused. Ahead of her was Camden Falls Elementary. She had visited it the week before. Min had taken her and Ruby there to meet their teachers and to make sure everything was in order. Still, Flora could suddenly hear her heart pounding in her ears again. She did not want to be the new kid, not even with Olivia and Nikki in her class. She hated doing anything that called attention to herself.

Flora let her breath out slowly and looked at the school. It was one storey tall and spread out in four directions from a centre point, forming a giant X. Behind the school was a car park that was filling up fast with cars, and to the side was a sprawling playground. In front was a lane where buses paused to let off their passengers.

"Let's wait for Nikki," said Flora, watching the buses.

"OK, but just for a couple of minutes," answered Olivia. "I told Mom and Dad I'd take Jack to his class."

"Mathias and I can do that," Lacey volunteered. "Travis and Jack are in the same room."

Olivia's brothers ran off with the Morrises, and Flora and Ruby and Olivia stood by the bus lane as kids streamed around them. Flora watched new backpacks and new sneakers and new notebooks and new jeans flash by. Kids laughed and called to one another, and every now and then, Olivia would wave or shout back. Flora thought then of Annika, her best friend from her old town; at this very moment, Annika was probably walking to school with Liza, who lived next door to Flora and Ruby's old house. Flora and Annika had spoken on the phone two nights earlier, and Flora knew what Annika would be wearing this morning, knew the colour of the backpack she had bought at Samson's, knew whose class Annika would be in. Flora wished mightily that she were standing between Annika and Liza right now. She could feel tears spring to her eyes and was wondering if she had any Kleenex with her when she heard Olivia shout, "Nikki! Over here!"

And there was Nikki, one of the last ones to step from her bus, holding tightly to Mae and pointedly ignoring the kid in front of them who jumped down the last step, holding his nose.

"Jerk," Olivia said in the kid's ear as he ran by her. He looked at her in surprise, then stuck out his tongue.

"Hi, you guys," said Nikki, trying to smile as Mae tugged at her hand and asked, "What was that boy doing? Why was he holding his nose?"

Nikki didn't answer her. She turned to her friends and said, "This is my little sister, Mae."

"Hi, Mae," said Ruby, Olivia and Flora.

Mae regarded the older girls with wide eyes, while Ruby stared at Mae's thin cotton dress, the rip under one arm, and the holes over each of the big toes of her sneakers. She also noticed that neither Nikki nor Mae wore a backpack.

"Mrs DuVane is going to take us shopping for school clothes," said Nikki, "but not until the weekend."

Ruby turned her gaze to the pavement, her face colouring.

The bell rang then, causing Olivia to exclaim, "We'd better go! Come on, you guys!"

This is it, thought Flora, and she stepped inside Camden Falls Elementary with her sister and her friends.

Five minutes later, after depositing Mae in her classroom, Flora, Olivia and Nikki said goodbye to Ruby, then entered Mrs Mandel's room.

Sixth grade had begun.

After no more than ten minutes with Mrs Mandel, Flora knew why she was the most popular teacher in the school. Mrs Mandel laughed often, smiled even more often, made jokes, and stood for absolutely no nonsense from her students. When a tall boy with lazy-looking eyes announced loudly that he refused to sit next to Nikki, Mrs Mandel said firmly, "George, in this class everyone is to be treated with respect. Also, I am in charge, and I make decisions, including who sits where. Now, please look at the front of the room. The chart by the window lists our classroom rules. I expect everyone to follow them. Would you please read the first rule aloud?"

George made a face. "'Treat others courteously'," he said.

"That includes not making faces," said Mrs Mandel. "Unless they are funny faces," she added, making a funny one herself, and the kids laughed.

Flora saw Nikki relax and felt herself relax, too.

As Mrs Mandel sat down behind her desk, Flora studied her. She tried to guess her teacher's age and decided she might be sixty. Younger than Min, but still getting a little old. Her wiry hair was grey, and wrinkles had formed around her eyes and mouth. She was plump, and on this first day of school had chosen to wear a blue-jean skirt (stretched tight over her belly), a pink cotton top and a pair of sandals.

After she had finished telling them what they would be studying that autumn, Mrs Mandel said,

"I want you to know that I have decided to retire next summer. So this will be my last year of teaching." Flora looked around as she heard several students gasp. "I know," Mrs Mandel continued. "I can't believe it myself. But I've been teaching here at Camden Falls Elementary for thirty-seven years."

"Wow," Olivia said softly.

Mrs Mandel smiled. "I even taught some of your parents. I taught your father, Sheldon. And your mother, Olivia. And yours, Flora."

"Really?" said Flora. "My mother?"

Mrs Mandel nodded. "In fact, she and Olivia's mother were in my class together when I taught fourth grade. So it's doubly nice to have the two of you together in my class this year."

And, thought Flora (who knew Olivia was thinking the same thing), we're doubly fortunate to be in your class before you retire.

"We should have a fun year," said Mrs Mandel. "In fact, this is going to be an interesting year for all of Camden Falls. Does anyone know why?"

A girl sitting behind Nikki raised her hand. "Because of the three hundred and fiftieth birthday celebration?" she said.

"That's right. Next spring, Camden Falls will be three hundred and fifty years old. I'm sure you've seen the signs posted around town. There's a lot of history in Camden Falls, and we want to celebrate that, as well as our identity. Our school is going to be very involved in the festivities. We plan on participating in an art show, a photography exhibit. . ."

For the next few minutes, Flora listened with interest as her teacher (her mother's teacher!) listed the activities in which CFE students could take part.

For a moment, just a moment, she felt as if she had lived here her entire life.

In the south hallway of Camden Falls Elementary, Ruby sat in her new classroom with her new teacher, Mr Lundy, and looked around at new faces. Mr Lundy had directed Ruby to a seat in the front row, which made Ruby suspect that he had spoken with the teachers from her old school and decided he needed to keep an eye on her.

Ruby did not know a single kid in her class, but she wasn't concerned. She knew she would make friends soon enough. And after school there were always Flora and Lacey and Olivia and sometimes Nikki.

Ruby, her attention wandering, refocused on Mr

Lundy when she heard him say, "And as part of the three hundred and fiftieth birthday celebration, our school is going to put on a play. It will be held in our auditorium and the proceeds from the sale of the tickets will go to the Camden Falls Historical Society."

Ruby shot her hand in the air. "A play?!" she exclaimed. "Who's going to be in it?"

"All the parts will be performed by students. There will be roles for students in every grade. The auditions will be held several weeks from now."

"And what's the play going to be about?" asked Ruby.

"About a unique chapter in Camden Falls's history," Mr Lundy replied. "Our very own witch trials."

"Like the Salem witch trials?" asked a boy.

Mr Lundy nodded.

Ruby grinned. School was getting off to a very good start. She couldn't wait until the final bell rang so she could find Flora and tell her that she, Ruby Jane Northrop, was going to star in the school play next spring in front of all of Camden Falls.

4

Aiken Avenue

"Min! Min!" cried Ruby as she and Flora burst through the door of Needle and Thread that afternoon. "Our school is going to put on a play and I'm going to star in it!"

"Land sakes," said Min. "Hold on a minute, Ruby." Min finished cutting three yards off a bolt of pinwale corduroy, folded the fabric neatly, placed it in a customer's basket and handed the customer a receipt. "There you go," she said. "Take this to the register whenever you're ready." Then Min turned to her granddaughters, who had shrugged off their backpacks and flung them on to one of the couches at the front of the store. "Now, what's all this?" she asked. "And how was the first day of school?"

"It was fine," said Flora. "How come you didn't

tell me that Mrs Mandel taught Mom in fourth grade?"

Min smiled. "I thought I'd let Mrs Mandel do that. Was it a nice surprise?"

"It was great. She taught Mom and Olivia's mom together."

"I remember," replied Min. "They had a very good year."

"This is going to be Mrs Mandel's last year of teaching," Flora added. "She's retiring over the summer."

"Ahem," said Ruby loudly.

Min turned to her younger granddaughter. "Now, what is this about a play?"

"Our school is going to put on a play for the birthday party next year, and I'm going to be in it!" said Ruby in a rush.

Min turned to Flora. "My stars. What is she talking about?"

Flora told Min about the activities that would be part of Camden Falls's birthday festivities. "One of them is going to be a play about witchcraft in colonial New England," Flora added.

"And you're going to be in the play?" Min asked Ruby.

"I'm going to star in it."

Min frowned. "Ruby," she said.

"All right. I don't know that yet. Mr Lundy said the auditions are going to be in a few weeks. But I'm sure I'll get the starring role."

"What is the starring role?" asked Flora. "Isn't it the part of an adult? And don't you think they'll give that to a sixth-grader?"

Ruby squirmed slightly. "Yes," she said. "I mean, no. I mean, the biggest part is one of the witches, and she *was* a grown-up. But no, they won't give that part to a sixth-grader. Not if I'm the best one who auditions."

"Ruby, I believe we need to have a little chat about modesty," said Min.

"And reality," Flora added under her breath.

Min glanced at Flora, then turned back to Ruby. "Another thing – do you know what the phrase 'Don't count your chickens before they hatch' means?"

"Don't think you're a beautiful chicken if you aren't?" Ruby guessed.

"Not exactly," replied Min. She looked up as the bell over the door jangled and Mary Woolsey entered Needle and Thread. "Good afternoon, Mary," said Min.

"'Afternoon, Min." Mary nodded to Ruby and

Flora before heading for her table at the back of the store. She was dressed in way too many clothes as usual, including a scarf and a jacket over what appeared to be two sweaters.

The bell jangled again as a customer entered. Min said, "Ruby, we'll continue this discussion tonight. I have to get back to work."

"Am I in trouble?" asked Ruby.

"No. I just want you to think about a few things."

"OK."

"Min?" said Flora. "Can Ruby and I go to Olivia's, please? Her parents are home. And we want to play outside with the kids."

"All right," said Min. "Have fun. Do you have any homework?"

"Just a little," said Ruby.

"Half an hour's worth," said Flora. "I can do it after supper."

With that, the Northrop girls left Needle and Thread and ran down Main Street.

When Robby's van pulled up in front of his house, he was surprised to see Alyssa, Travis, Mathias, Lacey, Ruby, Flora, Nikki, Olivia, Henry and Jack seated in a loose circle in the Walters' yard, Nikki's bicycle leaning against a tree.

"Hi, Robby!" called several of the kids as Robby stepped out of the van.

"Bye, Robby!" called the bus driver.

Robby didn't answer the kids or the driver. Instead, he headed for his house.

"Hey, Robby, what's wrong?" asked Olivia. "Come talk to us."

"OK, but first I have to tell my dad I'm home. It's the rule."

Robby stomped across his lawn and through his front door.

"I wonder what's the matter," said Olivia, staring after Robby.

The children shifted positions, breathing in the scents of tired grass, damp leaves and autumn flowers. Nikki pressed her hands together, then tucked them behind her knees. "Chilly," she said.

"It's almost fall!" exclaimed Alyssa. "We're going to learn all about fall in school. Halloween comes in the fall."

"So did you like preschool?" Olivia asked her.

"Yup."

"And she's very excited about going back tomorrow," added Lacey pointedly.

"In our class," spoke up Mathias, "we're going to learn about Camden Falls's history this year. Our teacher says she has old pictures of what the town used to look like. And also we're going to learn what it was like to live in a little town three hundred and fifty years ago. Did you know there were no cars or telephones and you had to go to the bathroom outside in this thing called an outhouse?"

"Ew," said Ruby.

"Mrs Mandel was telling us about all the stuff we can do for the celebration next year," said Olivia. "There's going to be a photography exhibit. I might try to take some pictures. I could take pictures of trees and insects, all the kinds that are here in Camden Falls."

"You should enter some things in the art show, Nikki," said Flora. "You're the best artist I know."

"Thank you," said Nikki, and she thought of her drawings, of the stacks and stacks of drawings that pleased her mother but for some reason annoyed her father.

"Well, are you?" Ruby asked Nikki.

"Am I what?"

"Going to enter anything in the art show?"

Nikki turned away from her friends and faced the Row Houses, the gorgeous Row Houses that made her small home seem shabby in comparison. It wasn't fair, thought Nikki. She and her mother, and sometimes Mae and Tobias, too, tried to make their house cheery. They kept the front stoop tidy. Nikki's mother planted flowers in the spring, if she was feeling up to it, and Nikki made wreaths for the front door. But these touches didn't repair the cracked window-panes or replace peeling paint. And no matter what the rest of the Shermans did, they couldn't stop Nikki's father from opening the front door and tossing paint cans and old appliances and broken motors and sometimes just plain trash into the garden for everyone to see.

"Nikki!" exclaimed Ruby in exasperation. Ruby never let one of her questions go unanswered.

"Oh," said Nikki. "Um, the art show. Well, I don't know. I mean, thank you. I'm glad you like my drawings. I'll ask my mom, I guess. . ."

"How come you have to ask—" Ruby started to say, then was stopped when Flora poked her in the back. Ruby let out a small squeal but didn't finish her question.

"Ruby, why don't you tell everyone about your dance lessons?" asked Flora a little too loudly.

Ruby looked sideways at her sister. "OK. Well, next week I'm finally going to start taking lessons again. I took tap and hip-hop and ballet in my other town."

41

"Cool," said Lacey.

"Now I'm going to go to Overlook Dance Studio for tap and hip-hop."

"Not ballet?" asked Olivia.

"I'm going to wait until the spring. Min says two classes are enough, especially if I get into the Children's Chorus. I'll be trying out for that soon."

"And especially if you get a part in the play," added Lacey.

Flora, who was relieved that Lacey hadn't said "the lead in the play", was studying her sister and thinking that Ruby was fitting into her new life here awfully easily – almost without regard for their old life – when Robby stamped out of his house and joined the kids on the lawn, looking no happier than he had when he'd got off the van.

Olivia scooted across the grass so that she was sitting directly in front of him. "What's the matter?" she asked.

Robby scowled down at the grass, then looked at the group of kids. "My class is moving," he said.

"Moving?" repeated Henry. "You mean to another room?"

"No." Robby's chin quivered. "To another school. To the *elementary school*."

"Oh!" cried Ruby. "Cool! You'll—"

"And I am *not* a little kid," Robby continued hotly. "I am seventeen. Other kids who are seventeen go to the high school. That is where I belong. Not at a school for *babies*."

Henry jumped to his feet. "Babies!" he cried. "I'm not—"

Olivia hushed her brother. "Why is your class moving?" she asked Robby.

"There isn't enough space for us at the high school. So they're getting rid of us."

"Oh, Robby," said Nikki. "They're not just getting rid of you. I'm sure they looked around until they found the right space for your class."

"No, they didn't," said Robby. "Because the right space is at the *high school*."

"Excuse me!" called a whispery voice then, and Olivia turned to see Mrs Willet, a letter in her hand, crossing the lawn towards the children. She was wearing her robe and slippers and tiptoeing along as if she didn't want to make any noise. "Could one of you nice youngsters direct me to the post office?" she asked.

Olivia jumped to her feet. "Mrs Willet," she said, "it's me, Olivia. Are you sure you want to go to the post office in your – I mean, um, you really need shoes if you're going to walk downtown."

Mrs Willet wasn't concerned about shoes. "I don't want anyone to see me," she whispered loudly. "They're all watching me, you know." She glanced up and down the street, which as far as Olivia could see was deserted except for the Row House kids.

Olivia caught Flora's eye and mouthed, "Get Mr Willet," which Flora did as quickly as she could. A minute later, he was hurrying towards his wife.

"Mrs Willet," Robby said as he watched Mr Willet approach, "you have to wear *clothes* and *shoes* when you go outside. That's the rule. *Clothes* and *shoes*. Mr Willet, Mrs Willet wasn't following the rule."

"It's OK, Robby," said Flora.

Mr Willet put his arm around his wife's waist. "Let's take a look at what you've got here. Ah. A letter to . . . your mother. OK. Well, Robby's right. You have to get dressed before you can go to the post office. So let's go back inside."

Ten minutes later, Min returned from work. As soon as the kids saw her, they ran to greet her. Then Nikki cried, "Oh, my gosh! What time is it?"

"Five-fifteen," said Olivia.

"I have to go!" Nikki jumped on to her bicycle and pedalled down Aiken Avenue, shouting over her shoulder, "See you at school tomorrow!"

"Bye!" called Olivia and Ruby and Flora.

"My school got changed," Robby said to Min, scowling again.

"I'm in preschool," announced Alyssa.

"Goodness me, there's a lot of news," said Min, lowering herself on to the porch step. "Tell me everything while I unwind from my day."

5

A Quiet Evening

For Flora Marie Northrop, the first two weeks of school at Camden Falls Elementary were a mix of the unfamiliar and the familiar, and Flora found the familiar more unsettling than the unfamiliar. How could anything, she wondered, feel familiar when nothing about her life was as it should be? At the beginning of the year, she had been living with her parents and Ruby in their old house in their old town. And she had been going to her old school with Annika and Liza. Now here she was living with Min and Ruby in Min's house in Camden Falls, going to a new school and making new friends. Sometimes as Flora sat in Mrs Mandel's room, she would catch herself turning to a page in a book or watching her teacher write on the board, and the moment would feel as familiar and comfortable as all the moments of her life up until the moment of the car accident. And this was what frightened Flora. Why should this new life already feel familiar? How could it feel familiar without her parents in it? And yet sometimes it did. And then Flora felt guilty.

September marched along, and the first day of autumn approached. The trees on Main Street took on a faded appearance, as though they had been through the wash once too often. Sometimes when Flora walked to school with her friends, she could smell wood smoke in the air. Overhead, Canada geese, flying in sloppy V-formation, honked shrilly.

One Friday evening, when supper was finished and the table had been cleared and the dishes loaded into the dishwasher, Min said, "My, it's chilly. I believe we need a fire tonight. We'll make the first fire of the season."

"Sweet!" exclaimed Ruby. "King Comma loves fires." She glanced at the black-and-white cat dozing in an armchair. "Min, does Daisy Dear like fires, too?"

Daisy Dear was Min's galumphing golden retriever who, despite her size, had many fears. She was afraid of the vacuum cleaner, afraid of thunder, and at first had also been afraid of King Comma.

"Well," said Min, "I think she sort of likes being with me when I sit in front of the fire, but if the fire pops or crackles, she leaves."

Ruby smiled. "Daisy is a 'fraidy dog."

"She certainly is," agreed Min.

Min made tea and Flora made hot chocolate for herself and Ruby. Soon they were settled in front of the fire in their cosy Row House. King moved so close to the fire that Flora wouldn't have been surprised if he'd started to melt. Daisy cautiously sat beside Min's chair and turned her back on the fireplace.

"Well, this is nice," said Min, looking at her granddaughters.

"And I don't even have any weekend homework," said Ruby.

"I have some," said Flora, "but only a little, and it's French, so that's fun."

Min smiled. "I remember when your mother and Olivia's mother started taking French in school. They would walk down Main Street, yabbering away a mile a minute, mostly saying nonsense words that sounded vaguely French. They hoped people would think they were actually foreign, even though everyone in town knew who they were."

Flora smiled and Ruby giggled.

"How old were they?" asked Ruby.

"About ten, I think."

The girls lay on the floor, first on their backs, then on their stomachs, gazing into the fire.

"Min?" said Ruby dreamily. "Will you help us with our Halloween costumes?"

"My word," said Min. "I know the store is already decorated for Halloween, but I still can't believe it'll be here so soon."

"And after that, Thanksgiving and then Christmas and then New Year's Eve," said Ruby.

A silence fell over the room. After a long moment, Min said, "I know what you're thinking, girls, and believe me, I've been thinking the same things."

"OK, what are we thinking?" Flora challenged her, sounding testy and regretting it.

Min leaned over and tweaked the toe of one of Flora's slippered feet. "You're thinking about the holidays and wondering what they're going to be like this year, the first ones without your parents. And you're wondering how we're going to celebrate. Maybe you're even wondering if we should celebrate at all. Is that right?"

Flora lowered her chin on to her arms. "Yup. That's exactly what I was thinking. How did you know?"

"Because that's what I've been thinking. Things are going to be different for me, too. After your grandfather died, I stopped spending the holidays at home – partly because it was too sad, and partly so I could be with my family. I've been going to your house for Thanksgiving for so long that I've forgotten how to prepare a turkey. I haven't had Thanksgiving at home in ages. I haven't had Christmas here, either, since I usually spend it with your aunt."

"Aunt Allie?" asked Ruby. Aunt Allie was the younger sister of Flora and Ruby's mother.

"Mm-hmm," said Min.

"Where does she live?" asked Ruby. "I forget."

"In New York City. She's a writer."

"Did she and Mom not get along?" asked Flora. "We've only met Aunt Allie, like, twice."

"They weren't close," said Min carefully. "They're very different people."

"Is Aunt Allie the person who would take care of Ruby and me if anything ever happened to you?" asked Flora.

"Maybe," said Min. "But, Flora, please don't start worrying about that again. I promise I will work things out so that you girls will always be taken care of."

Flora scowled, then said, "So you always go to

New York for Christmas? Does that mean we have to go there, too? I don't want to spend Christmas in New York City."

"Let's not think that far ahead," replied Min. "Let's just get through Halloween. Halloween is fun here. You haven't experienced Halloween in Camden Falls. You can go trick-or-treating on Main Street."

"On Main Street?" Ruby repeated in dismay. "You mean we don't go trick-or-treating at people's houses here?"

"You can do that, too. But you can also go in town. All the stores stay open, and the store owners dress up in costumes and hand out candy. Gigi and I usually have to get fifty bags of candy to make sure we have enough for everyone who comes into town."

"You mean *you* wear a costume on Halloween?" said Ruby.

"I most certainly do. So does Gigi. We made the costumes ourselves. I'm the Wicked Witch of the West from *The Wizard of Oz* and Gigi is Glinda, the Good Witch."

Flora rolled over and faced Ruby. "Maybe *we* should be characters from *The Wizard of Oz*. Nikki and Olivia, too. We could be Dorothy, the Tin Man, the Scarecrow and the Cowardly Lion."

"Cool!" said Ruby.

The fire popped loudly then, and Daisy fled from the living room in terror.

"Speaking of events that are coming up," said Min, her eyes following Daisy, "I know someone who has a birthday right around the corner."

"Olivia," said Flora.

"The big one-oh," added Ruby.

"Is that what she calls it?" asked Min, laughing.

"Yup. She's really excited about her birthday. She wants a big party for the big one-oh."

"Min, do you think her parents will be able to have a big party for her?" asked Flora. "I mean, since Mr Walter lost his job?"

"Well, I don't know."

"Maybe we could give Olivia a *surprise* party!" exclaimed Flora.

"Yes!" cried Ruby. "A surprise party! That would be so much fun. Nikki could help us."

"We could invite our friends from school and from the Row Houses," added Flora.

"And everybody could jump out and yell 'Surprise!' like on TV," said Ruby. "That would be so cool. Maybe Olivia would faint."

"Good gracious me," said Min. "I'm not sure we want that. But a surprise party is a lovely idea."

Ruby stood up and said, "I'm going to go to my room and write down some surprise-party ideas." She clumped up the stairs.

Flora gazed into the fire again, and her thoughts twisted and turned all by themselves. Suddenly, she found herself thinking about Scary Mary Woolsey. "Min," said Flora, "wait right here. There's something I want to show you. It's in my room. I'll be back in just a minute."

When Flora returned to the living room and Min's bright fire, she was carrying the photo she had shown Olivia, the photo of her mother posing with Mary Woolsey. Flora perched on the arm of Min's chair and held out the picture.

"What's this?" asked Min as she put on her reading glasses.

"I found it," said Flora. "In the attic. I was just looking around up there one day. . ." Her voice trailed off and she turned the photo over so Min could see the writing on the back.

"'Frannie and Mary – nineteen seventy,'" read Min.

"At first I thought 'Mary' meant your sister," said Flora. "Mary Elizabeth. But then I realized this is a picture of Mary Woolsey. See the necklace she's wearing?"

"Well, I'll be," said Min. "It *is* Mary Woolsey."

"I didn't know you knew her that long ago. Do you remember when this picture was taken? I mean, why was she posing with Mom? Mary didn't work for you then, did she?"

"No. There was no Needle and Thread back then."

"That's what I thought. So what *did* Mary Woolsey do? Didn't she . . . didn't she just live by herself in that little house and never come out? It seems weird that she would pose with Mom."

Min frowned, staring at the picture, and Flora was relieved that her grandmother hadn't asked her why she'd been hunting around in the attic. "Frannie was four," murmured Min. "That must have been . . . land sakes, I wonder if this was taken on the day . . . yes, I believe it was."

"What? Taken on what day?"

"The day Mary showed up at our house to say thank you for what my father had done to help her. She didn't know how to reach my parents, but she knew I was still living in our old house, so she came here. In fact, my parents had moved to Florida, and my father had died several years earlier."

"She wanted to thank your father? Lyman Davis?" Flora thought back to the letters she had also found

54

in the box of papers. Lyman Davis, she had read, had made something of a bad name for himself after the stock market crash in 1929, which was several years before Min was born. He had been a wealthy stockbroker in Camden Falls, and from what Flora could piece together, had made investments that had lost money for his clients. In fact, many of them lost their entire fortunes, plunging them into poverty during the Depression. Min's father had left his job, a move his former friends (and some of his relatives) viewed as cowardly, and the family then lived mainly on a large inheritance that had come to Min's mother. "What did your father do for Sca – for Mary?" asked Flora.

"You know, I don't remember. This was decades ago, honey," said Min. "My father was always doing nice things for people, though, and lots of times he never said anything about it. He just went ahead and lent people money or quietly did favours."

"Lent people money?" repeated Flora. "I thought he lost all his money in nineteen twenty-nine."

"Now, where did you hear about that?"

"In some letters I found in the attic," Flora admitted.

"Oh," said Min. "There's an awful lot of old stuff up there, that's for sure. Well, let me see. Yes, Dad did have a bad time for a while. Of course, that was before I was born. But our family got back on its feet. Dad never worked again but Mother had money, and Dad still had some of his own. I think my parents felt guilty that their lives didn't change much after the crash, even though the lives of so many of Dad's clients changed dramatically. For the worse. But as the years went by, things settled down. Anyway, maybe that's why Dad did so much for other people – because he felt bad about what had happened after the crash. So when Mary showed up at our door wanting to thank my father, I wasn't surprised, even though I didn't know he had helped her out."

"But what about the picture?" asked Flora.

"The picture," said Min. "Well, I think it was just that Mary was so shy and awkward, and I wanted her to feel more comfortable. So I invited her in and offered her tea or something, and your mother kept running through the living room, where we were talking, and Mary kept saying how appreciative she was, so finally I asked if Mary wouldn't like me to take her picture with your mother. I told her I'd send it to *my* mother along with a letter about Mary's visit."

"But you *didn't* send the picture," Flora pointed out.

"I guess not. Or maybe this one is a copy. Maybe I took two to make certain we had one good one. I really don't remember, honey. I'm sorry."

"Huh," said Flora, settling down in front of the fire. She had the feeling that someone had just read her the first page of a fascinating book and then slammed the cover shut.

6

The Big One-oh

Next door to Flora, on that same chilly, blustery evening, Olivia Walter sat in front of her computer and began composing a list. It was headed: *Wild Mammals I Have Seen in Camden Falls*. Olivia wound a curl of hair around her finger, then typed: red squirrel, grey squirrel, eastern chipmunk, bat, opossum, porcupine, deer mouse, white-footed mouse, cottontail rabbit, red fox, white-tailed deer, eastern mole. Before the list was finished, she abandoned it and started a second one: *Birds I Have Seen in Camden Falls* – black-capped chickadee, pileated woodpecker, house wren, blue jay, slate-colored junco, northern cardinal (male and female), eastern bluebird, sparrow (not sure what kind), duck, goose, chicken. Leaving that list unfinished, too, she began a third: *Insects I Have Seen in Camden*

Falls – butterflies (varied), ladybird, mosquito, flea, bee (honey and queen), wasp, hornet, gnat, flies (varied), daddy longlegs. She was about to start a fourth list, for spiders, when she realized she didn't know the names of many spiders.

"Huh," she said aloud. "I'd better read up on spiders."

"Are you talking to yourself again, Olivia?" called Henry from his room.

"No!" Olivia called back. She left her computer and lay down on her bed. She wondered if trying to capture Camden Falls wildlife for the photography exhibit was too big a project.

"Of course, I don't have to photograph *every* kind of animal," she said. "And I've left out reptiles and fish—"

"I can hear you! You *are* talking to yourself!" said Henry.

Olivia rolled off her bed and very quietly closed the door to her room. She knew her brother was just teasing her, but she didn't feel like being teased. She also didn't feel like having a fight with Henry.

Olivia stood in the very centre of her room. She did this sometimes. Standing in the centre, she could feel the presence of her neighbours. She shared one wall of her room with Ruby's next door. Across the hallway, one wall of Jack's room shared a wall with a room in Mr Pennington's house. And in front of Olivia was her window, which faced on to Aiken Avenue. Olivia rested her elbows on the sill and stared outside. In the dim glow from the porch light, she could make out her garden with the little flower bed that Olivia herself had planted. To the right was Min's tidy garden with its magnolia tree, the one Olivia's mother remembered climbing with Flora and Ruby's mother when they were young. "We would hide up there and drop water balloons down on Allie," she had said once.

Olivia smiled at the thought that she and Flora and Ruby were growing up in the Row Houses just as her mother and Frannie and Allie had grown up here. But, she reminded herself, my family might not be living here if it weren't for Mr Pennington. Olivia's mother had said many times that Mr Pennington had bravely paved the way for people of colour in the Row Houses. The first time she had mentioned that, Olivia hadn't understood what she meant. "What do you mean, paved the way for people of colour?" she had asked.

"These houses are old, very old," her mother had told her.

"I know. They were built before you were born."

"Good heavens, they were built before *Min* was born. Long before she was born. They were built in the eighteen hundreds. And for decades, closer to a century, actually, the only people who lived here were white. Mr Pennington and his wife were the first people of colour to buy one of the Row Houses, and apparently this made quite a stir in Camden Falls. But the Penningtons were respected. Mr Pennington was a teacher at Camden Falls Elementary back then, and eventually he became principal of the high school. So when my parents bought one of the Row Houses a few years later, it wasn't such a big deal. And by the time the Morrises and then the Fongs moved in, no one thought twice about it."

Olivia, still gazing out of her window, thought about Mr Pennington and how brave he had been. She couldn't imagine being treated the way she suspected he and his wife had been treated. Kids at school sometimes teased Olivia, but not because of her skin colour. They called her "Professor" since she was smart, and "baby" since she was a good year younger than most of the other kids in her class. Olivia didn't mind these names. She liked being smart, and she couldn't help having skipped a grade. If kids wanted to tease her about those things, well, that was their choice. Personally, Olivia thought it was a waste of valuable time.

Olivia returned to her desk and looked at her calendar. She counted the days to her birthday, which she had marked with a sticker in the shape of a cupcake over which she had written TEN, and under which she had written THE BIG 1-0!!!! All summer, Olivia had dreamed of a lavish birthday party the likes of which had never been seen in the Walter household. Olivia felt she could reasonably petition for one, though. She had said to her parents, "I know no one in our family has ever had a party like this, but ten is a big deal. It's the first age with two numbers in it. Maybe this could be the beginning of a tradition. A Walter family tenth-birthday tradition. I'll have the first big party, then Henry, then Jack." This, she hoped, made her sound slightly less greedy, as if she were thinking not so much of herself as of her brothers, and of the Walter family in general.

"We'll see," her parents had said.

That was before Mr Walter was laid off from his job. Olivia had not asked about a big party since then, although she still longed for one. She also had not dared to ask for the birthday present for which she longed: a pet. The Walters had no pets, and

Olivia was desperate for one. Flora and Ruby had King Comma and Daisy Dear. Mr Pennington had Jacques. The Willets had Sweetie, the Malones had two cats, the Fongs had two dogs, and the Morrises had two hamsters and a guinea pig. But pets weren't cheap. Even if you got one for free, you had to buy food and toys and other supplies, and then there were the vet bills. Olivia's parents had said they would be all right for a while without jobs, but Olivia knew this was not a wise time to ask for something that would add to their expenses.

Olivia sighed. She had thought that the big one-oh would mark the start of a fabulous time in her life. But a lot of things were going to have to change, and change quickly, in order for that to happen. She felt unsettled. Her father didn't have a job. He talked of starting his own business now, which was exciting, but he wasn't sure what he wanted to do. Olivia's mother didn't have a job, either, and soon one or the other of her parents would need to work. Then there was Mr Pennington. For quite a while now, Olivia had been keeping a secret for him. Only Olivia knew that old Mr Pennington was having a bit of trouble taking care of himself. Olivia had been giving him a hand – checking on him, pitching in with his housework, making sure he remembered to care for

Jacques, lock his doors, turn off the oven and a hundred other things. But she couldn't always be there for him, so she knew this arrangement wasn't right. And Mr Pennington feared that if anyone else found out what was going on, he would be made to move to a nursing home, which he couldn't face. "Not after forty-five years here. This is my home. I can't leave it," he had said to Olivia. And Olivia didn't want him to leave it. She couldn't imagine the Row Houses without Mr Pennington next door.

Olivia had just slumped on to her bed when she heard the phone ring. Moments later, a knock sounded on her door, and Olivia's father said, "For you," and opened the door just wide enough to hand the phone through it to Olivia.

"Thanks," said Olivia. Then, "Hello?"

"Hi, it's me!" said Flora.

Flora, Olivia thought, sounded excited. "What's going on?" she asked.

"Oh, I don't know. Hey, Olivia?"

"Yeah?"

"About your birthday?"

"Yeah?"

"Well, I guess you're going to have a party, aren't you?"

"I guess so. I don't really know. But if I do have

one, don't worry, you'll be invited. You and Ruby and Nikki."

"And who else? I mean, who else would you want to have at your party if you have one?"

"My brothers," replied Olivia. "And Mr Pennington. And everyone in the Row Houses. And—" Olivia caught herself. This was the guest list for the giant one-oh birthday party she had hoped for. "But I can't really do that, I know. That's too many people."

"Not necessarily," said Flora.

"What?"

"I mean, well, you should, um, ask whoever you want to your party."

"But Mom and Dad can't afford a big party now."

"OK. Well, if you were planning your dream party—"

"My dream party?"

"Come on, Olivia. Just play along. Don't you like to pretend? Pretend you could have any kind of party you wanted. *Any* kind. What would it be?"

Olivia lay back against her pillows and stared at the ceiling. "OK. I'd invite the people I just told you about, plus the girls in our class and my cousins. All the decorations would be pink and silver. The cake would be pink, too, with silver decorations, and on top would be those big number candles – a one and a zero." Olivia stopped speaking. "Are you working on your computer? You sound like you're typing."

"No! No, I'm not. Now what would the decorations be?"

"I'm not sure. Maybe . . . giant butterflies. Are you *sure* you aren't writing this down or something?"

Flora ignored the question. "And what do you want most of all for your birthday? What would be the perfect gift?"

"A pet," said Olivia instantly. "Any pet at all."

Teddy Bears

"Bye! Wish me luck!" called Ruby.

"Good luck," said Flora and Min as Ruby ran across the lawns to the Morrises' house. And Min added, "Break a leg!"

"Do you think she'll get in?" Flora asked her grandmother as they walked to Needle and Thread. It was early on a brisk October Saturday morning, and Flora was feeling pensive. Today was the day of the first teddy bear class, but Ruby wouldn't be there, because today was also the day of the tryouts for the Camden Falls Children's Chorus. Lacey Morris was trying out, too, and Mrs Morris had offered to take Ruby along to the auditions.

"Get into the chorus?" said Min. "Well, I don't know. She does have a beautiful voice, and she's been in a chorus before, so I suppose her chances are good. It depends on the competition. I suspect, though, that the director of the chorus will try to take on as many truly interested children as she can." Min paused. "Ruby is going to be awfully busy between her dance classes and the chorus."

"And the play," Flora reminded Min. "Don't forget about that. I'm sure she'll get a part in the play."

"Sakes alive. I hope she's going to be able to find time to do her homework."

Flora scuffed through the leaves on Aiken Avenue, thinking of Ruby – and of Ruby's classes and activities and all the people she'd meet and how she was fitting into life in Camden Falls as if the town were a jigsaw puzzle missing a piece, and Ruby was that piece, and Camden Falls had just been waiting for her to come along.

Where does that leave me? Flora wondered.

Flora and Min turned on to Main Street and Flora said, "Ruby's going to miss the very first teddy bear class."

"I know," said Min, "but I don't think she minds. You know she doesn't care much for sewing. Not the way you do."

"But she helped plan the classes. And she helped

Olivia and Nikki and me get all the materials ready."

"So you think she should be here today?"

"I just think she could care a little more."

Min stopped walking and took Flora by the hand. "What is this really about, honey?" she asked. "Is it about Ruby not participating, or is it something else? I know what the teddy bears meant to you and Ruby after the accident."

Flora bit her lip and looked past Min at Main Street. "I don't even think Ruby cares about her bear any more. She still has it, but it's jammed in the back of her closet."

"Do you think that because Ruby doesn't need her bear and she's getting involved in so many activities here, she's forgetting about your other life – and your parents?" asked Min.

"I don't know." Flora pulled her hand from Min's. "Let's just go," she said. "Olivia and I have to get everything set up. The class starts in an hour."

Feeling crabby, and not liking herself for feeling crabby when Min was trying to understand things and be helpful, Flora marched ahead of her grandmother and threw open the door to Needle and Thread. Then she marched past Gigi to the class table at the back of the store and began setting out the kits that she and Olivia and Nikki and Ruby had worked so hard to assemble.

"Good morning, Flora!" Gigi called pointedly from her seat at the register.

"Hi." Flora kept her eyes on her work. But she could hear Gigi say to Min, "Bad morning?" and Min reply, "I'll tell you later."

Flora examined one of the kits. The girls and Gigi and Min had decided that in order to save time (since making an entire teddy was a big project, and each class was only several hours long), most of the main parts of the teddies should be cut out before the classes began. So Flora, Olivia, Nikki and Ruby had cut out the pieces for teddy legs, arms, tails, bodies and heads, leaving details such as noses to be decided on and cut out later by the students. Flora, Olivia and Gigi, who would be teaching the classes, would show the students how to stitch together and stuff the smaller pieces and then help them attach them to the bodies. After that, the kids could make the faces of their choice, using buttons, felt and embroidery thread.

Flora, standing back from the table and looking at the eight teddy kits, one each in front of eight folding chairs, couldn't help but feel a surge of excitement. This was how she felt when she began any project.

She would look at a new skein of yarn and a pair of knitting needles, or at a stamp pad, rubber stamps, paper, ribbons, fancy braids and everything she needed to make a greeting card, and feel a small thrill, a skip in her heart, as she imagined taking the very first step towards creating something all her own.

Flora let out a satisfied sigh and turned back to Min and Gigi.

Fifteen minutes before the class was to begin, Robby strode into Needle and Thread, followed by his father.

"I'm here, Flora!" he announced. "Here to make a teddy for a kid in need. Only I want to give my teddy to Mrs Willet."

Flora opened her mouth, then closed it. She understood why Robby wanted to give his bear to Mrs Willet, but Min and Gigi had promised to give all the finished teddies to Helping Hand, a Camden Falls group dedicated to helping children in need. Flora raised her eyebrows at Gigi, but Gigi just smiled at Robby and said, "First let's concentrate on making your bear. Have you done any sewing, Robby?"

"My mom showed me how to sew on buttons,

and sometimes she lets me use her sewing machine."

"Robby's pretty good with the sewing machine," spoke up Mr Edwards.

"Excellent," said Gigi. "Why don't you go on back and choose a place at the table? The others should be here in a few minutes."

Olivia arrived then, breathless, and said, "Wow, Flora, you got everything set up already."

"We just need the name tags," replied Flora. Then she added in a whisper, "Are you nervous?"

"A little," admitted Olivia. "I've never taught a class before."

"Me, neither," said Flora.

"I'm glad Gigi will be helping us."

"Let's pass out the name tags," said Flora. She reached for the stack of tags she and Olivia had made and decorated the day before, shuffled through them, and handed Robby his. "Here, put this on," she instructed him.

Robby regarded the tag. "But you already know who I am," he said.

"I know, but some of the other kids won't. If we're all wearing tags, then we'll all know each other's names. Even Olivia and Gigi and I are going to wear tags."

"OK." Robby fastened the name tag to his shirt. "Who else is in the class?" he asked.

Flora handed him the cards.

"Kirsten," Robby read slowly, sounding out the word. "Violet, Melanie, Lydia. Hey, is that Lydia Malone?"

"Yup," said Flora.

Robby frowned. "Lydia was mean to Nikki," he said.

"Yes, but Lydia's trying very hard to be nice now. Wasn't she nice when she babysat for you?"

Robby shuffled his feet. "Yes." Then he added quietly, "Even though I'm not a baby."

Flora felt her cheeks grow hot. "I know, Robby. I'm sorry. I didn't mean to hurt your feelings. Look. Let's see what other names are here. This one says Jade. I don't know who she is. But these say Henry and Mathias. And here they come," said Flora.

"Here comes just about everybody," added Olivia. She was looking at the stream of kids who were heading for the table while their parents perched on the couches and began to talk quietly.

"I see Henry and Mathias!" exclaimed Robby. "And there's Lydia," he added.

"And I think that's Melanie," said Flora. "She's in Ruby's class in school."

Flora watched the kids hesitantly take seats around the table. The ones who were friends sat next to each other – Henry and Mathias, Violet and Kirsten. Robby eyed Lydia, then sat on the other side of Mathias.

Flora glanced at Gigi, who gave her a nod as if to say, "This is your class. You lead the way."

"OK. Um, hi. Hi, everyone," said Flora. "Well, um, some of you already know me. My name is Flora Northrop. And this is Olivia Walter. And this is Olivia's grandmother."

"You can call me Gigi," Gigi spoke up, pointing to her name tag. "Welcome, everybody."

"We're going to be teaching this class," Flora continued.

"Do you all know what we're here to do?" asked Olivia.

"Make teddy bears?" said Jade.

"That's right. You're going to learn to sew by making teddies. Then the bears will be given to kids who really need them."

"How many of you have done any sewing?" asked Gigi. "Any sewing at all?"

Robby, Lydia, Violet and Kirsten raised their hands.

"Great," said Gigi. "And it's also fine if you're a beginner."

"Look at the things in your teddy bear kit now," said Flora. "Take out all the pieces and spread them in front of you. You should have two pieces for each arm, two for each leg—"

"I didn't know bears had arms," said Violet. "I thought they had four legs."

"OK. Well, we're going to call their front legs their arms. You should also have two pieces for the tail," said Flora, "two for the body, and two for the head. We'll talk about noses and eyes and ears later."

"The first thing we're going to do," said Olivia, "is sew together each arm and leg, then stuff it with fiberfill."

"And did you know," said Flora, "that when you sew things together, you almost always put the *right* sides together, then turn your piece inside out after you've stitched it?"

"Why?" asked Melanie.

"Because that way the seam winds up on the inside," Flora told her. "You don't see it. It's almost like magic."

The students set to work pinning the pieces together and taking turns at the sewing machines. Flora, Olivia and Gigi bustled among the kids, helping with the machines, occasionally ripping out seams, demonstrating how to turn curved edges, and offering encouragement, especially to Robby and Melanie, who became frustrated quickly.

Flora was surprised to look at the clock later and find that an hour had gone by. "Let's take a break," she said.

The kids wandered around the store, and Flora sat for a moment with Min, who was talking to some customers.

"Needle and Thread," Min was saying, "is going to have an exhibit of antique quilts during the birthday celebration next spring. I think we'll have a float in the parade, too. We'll be wearing costumes that we'll make ourselves. . ."

Flora looked around at the bustling store. The kids, without being told, were already drifting back to the table and setting to work again. Mary Woolsey had arrived and was conferring with customers. Min jumped up to help someone choose a pattern.

"Flora! Can you please come here?" called Jade. "I think I'm ready to sew the arms and legs to the body."

Flora smiled. Here at Needle and Thread, in the midst of fabric and projects and sewing machines, she almost felt at home.

*

Several hours later, at the end of Needle and Thread's first teddy bear class, eight proud students stood back to admire eight finished teddies.

"Beautiful!" Gigi pronounced. "Absolutely beautiful!"

"Hey, Dad!" Jade called, and her father, seated on one of the couches, swivelled around. "Look what I did!" Jade held up her bear. "And he's going to be a present for someone who needs him."

"Why, he's wonderful," Jade's father was saying when the door flew open and Ruby and Lacey hurtled into the store.

"I'm in the chorus!" Ruby cried. "We both are! Lacey got in, too!"

"My stars and garters," exclaimed Min, "what wonderful news!" Min turned to Flora. "Isn't that wonderful news?"

"Yes," said Flora. "Wonderful."

"Flora? Can I please give my bear to Mrs Willet? *Please?*" Robby stood before Flora, holding out his finished teddy. "I think she needs him."

Flora, watching her beaming sister accept praise and congratulations, felt as if she were spinning up and away until she hovered above the crowd of people in Needle and Thread, until she hovered above Main Street and Camden Falls. She looked down at her sister and thought she could almost see the puzzle piece snap into place.

"Flora?" said Robby again.

"OK. You can give your bear to Mrs Willet," said Flora, and she turned and walked out the back door to stand in the alley and take deep breaths until the threat of tears had disappeared.

Ghosts and Goblins

The autumn days were growing shorter, sunrise later each morning and sunset earlier each afternoon. "Darker at both ends," Min remarked. On some days, by the time Ruby came home from a dance class or a chorus rehearsal, it was already twilight.

"Remember at the beginning of the summer when it was still light at nine o'clock?" asked Flora.

She and Olivia and Nikki were sitting in Olivia's yard after school one day.

"In three weeks, we'll set our clocks back," said Olivia. "Then the days will really end early."

"I like the short, dark days," said Flora.

"Not me," said Nikki. "I'd rather be outside."

"You know what else happens in three weeks?" asked Olivia. "Halloween. I can't believe it's already Halloween again. What are you guys going to be?"

Nikki shrugged. "It doesn't matter. I never go trick-or-treating."

"What?!" exclaimed Olivia. "What do you mean?"

"I mean I never go trick-or-treating."

"You've never been once in your whole life?"

Nikki shook her head. "We live way out in the country. There's no place to go trick-or-treating."

"Don't you go in town?" asked Olivia. "That's why the stores stay open late on Halloween. So everyone will have a safe place for trick-or-treating."

Nikki squirmed. "My dad doesn't approve of Halloween."

"I don't get it," said Olivia. "Doesn't—"

Flora nudged Olivia's foot with her sneaker. "Olivia," she said.

"But I really want to know," replied Olivia. "Doesn't Mae go trick-or-treating? Have you guys ever even worn costumes? What do you do if your teacher says you can bring your costume to school for a Halloween party? How come your father doesn't approve?"

Nikki stared across the street. "I guess it isn't that he doesn't approve. It's more like he just doesn't want us to have any fun. . ." Nikki's voice trailed off.

"But that's—" Olivia started to say.

"Olivia, I really don't want to talk about it."

Flora turned to Nikki. "Do you think you could secretly come trick-or-treating with us this year?"

Nikki turned pale. "No! Are you kidding? If I got caught doing something like that, I – I—"

"Nikki, it's OK. Never mind," said Flora. "It was just an idea. What about talking to your father? What if you told him we really, really want you to come with us?"

"Maybe," said Nikki.

"Hey, here comes Robby," said Olivia, looking down the row of houses.

"And Ruby and Lacey," added Flora, looking in the other direction.

Presently, as often happened at the Row Houses, all the kids except for the Malone sisters soon gathered.

"What are you guys doing?" asked Robby, and Ruby thought he sounded sullen. What had happened to the cheerful Robby she knew?

"Talking about Halloween," said Olivia.

"Huh. That's for babies."

"Well, then I'm a baby," said Olivia, "because I really like Halloween."

"What are you going to be this year?" Mathias asked her.

Olivia frowned. "I'm still deciding."

"I'm going to be a ghost," said Alyssa.

"A ghost!" exclaimed Henry. "Can't you be more original?"

"Well, I wanted to be something else, but my mom said no."

"What did you want to be?" asked Robby.

"A piece of cake."

Flora laughed. "That would be a little hard. But I bet we could make you into a cupcake."

"Or a candle," said Olivia.

"A candle?" Alyssa grinned. "I like that."

"How would you make her into a candle?" asked Ruby.

"Simple. Put her in a pink leotard and make her a yellow flame hat," Olivia replied.

Nikki smiled.

"I want to be Bugs Bunny," said Jack.

"I want to be a firefighter," said Travis.

"What about you?" Ruby asked Robby. "Are you going to go trick-or-treating?"

"I don't know. Maybe."

"Hey, everybody!" called a cheerful voice.

"Oh, no." Robby let out a groan.

"Robby, it's *Lydia*," said Olivia. "What's the matter?" She stood up and waved to Lydia, who was striding down Aiken Avenue.

"Hi, Robby," said Lydia. She shrugged off her backpack and set it on the pavement. "Let me just stick this in my house, then I'll go tell your mother I'm here. I hope she didn't think I was going to be late."

"Late for what?" asked Lacey.

"Babysitting for Robby."

"I told you – I. AM. NOT. A. BABY." Robby turned a furious face on Lydia. "Didn't I tell you that?"

"Robby, I – I'm sorry. Really." Lydia looked helplessly at Olivia.

Ruby remembered the many late-summer days when she had seen Robby and Lydia happily walking into town or reading under the ancient maple tree in the Edwardses' garden.

"All right, look, Robby," said Lydia. "Stay here with the other kids for a few minutes and I'll be right back."

Lydia disappeared into her house, then reappeared and dashed across the gardens towards Robby's. As she did so, Robby muttered, "And I'm not a kid, either."

"Hey!" exclaimed Henry. "I know what I want to be for Halloween – a pirate."

"Ooh! Ooh! We have an eye patch you can wear!" exclaimed Lacey.

The younger kids ran to the Morrises' house, leaving Flora, Nikki and Olivia sitting in the Walters' garden, knees drawn up to their chins. Robby sat alone on Olivia's front steps.

"Hey, you guys. I never told you about the great idea I had," said Flora. She glanced behind her at Robby, who looked away from her.

"What great idea?" asked Nikki.

"Min was telling Ruby and me how every Halloween she dresses like the Wicked Witch of the West from *The Wizard of Oz* and Gigi dresses like Glinda. So I thought maybe the three of us and Ruby could be Dorothy, the Tin Man, the Cowardly Lion and the Scarecrow." She glanced over her shoulder again. "We need someone to be the Wizard," she added. "I wonder who that could be."

Robby glared off into the distance.

"But," said Nikki, "I don't know if I can dress up. Like I said."

"It's OK. It was just an idea."

"If I can, though," Nikki went on, "Mae will probably have to come trick-or-treating with me. I couldn't leave her behind."

"Mae could be Toto!" cried Olivia.

"Well. . ." said Nikki.

"Do you really think you might be able to come?" asked Flora.

"Maybe."

"We don't want you to get in trouble," added Olivia.

Nikki let out a huge sigh. "If I'm going to ask about this, I'll have to do it very carefully. I'll talk to Mom first." She sighed again. "The problem is that Mom can't really stand up to my father."

"I'm back!" said Lydia. "Robby, your mother's leaving now. She said your dad will be home in two hours. Guess what. We get to start dinner. What do you want to make?"

Robby brightened. "Can we have pizza?"

"Frozen pizza? Sure. We'll make a salad, too, OK?"

"OK."

Lydia sat on the lawn with Olivia and Nikki and Flora. Every so often a maple leaf drifted to the ground. Lydia sniffed the air. "Smells good," she said. "Isn't it weird how you can actually smell the seasons? You know – how spring smells different from summer, and autumn has its own smell, and winter smells like snow, even though snow doesn't have a smell?"

"Mmm," said Flora.

85

"Robby, come join us." Lydia patted the ground beside her.

"All right." Robby left the steps and plopped on to the grass between Nikki and Lydia.

Around them, Ruby and Lacey and Henry and Jack and Travis and Mathias and Alyssa ran and shouted and laughed.

"A firefighter needs a hose!"

"I know what we can make your flame hat out of – felt."

"Who has a wand? I need a wand!"

"Maybe I should be a princess instead. That way, I would get to wear a crown and oh, oh! I could wear my ballet slippers!"

Robby looked seriously at Lydia for several moments. At last he said, "Lydia, could you please not call me a kid? Or talk about babysitting?"

"OK," said Lydia. "But, Robby, won't you tell me what's wrong? You never minded when I sat for you before."

"That was when I went to high school. Now I go to the little kids' school again. It just . . . makes me feel like a baby."

"Oh," said Lydia. "I see."

"Are *you* going to go trick-or-treating?" Robby asked her.

"Well . . . no."

"Are you going to wear a costume?"

Lydia looked at the ground and flushed. "Um, I don't know. I got asked to this Halloween party. But I'm probably not going to go."

Flora glanced at Nikki and Olivia, and Olivia raised her eyebrows.

"OK, here's the thing, Robby," said Lydia. "Halloween is a fun holiday. You should do whatever you want. If you want to get dressed up, you should. If you want to go trick-or-treating, you should. Don't worry about what other people think."

"That's easy for you to say," muttered Robby.

"Not really," replied Lydia.

"Flora! Flora! Can you sew me a flame hat?" cried Alyssa as she ran out of Olivia's house. "Ruby said you're really good at sewing."

"Can you sew a penguin head?" asked Travis.

"I'm going to need a tail," said Jack.

"I'll try anything," said Flora.

9

The Witches of Camden Falls

When Ruby Northrop entered a room, people usually noticed. Ruby was used to this and made the most of her entrances. On the day of the auditions for the school play, Ruby strode through the door of her classroom, smiling.

"Hi, Ruby! Hi, Ruby!" called several voices.

"Hello!" Ruby waved to her classmates.

Ava Longyear, who was already seated at her desk, jumped up and ran to greet Ruby. "The auditions are today. Are you really going to try out for the biggest part?"

"Yup," said Ruby. "I definitely want to be Alice Kendall."

"Ooh, the worst witch," said Ava.

"But that's just the thing. She wasn't a witch at all," said Ruby, who had read the script for the play several times and had listened carefully when Mr Lundy talked to her class about witches and witchcraft in New England in the 1600s. A handful of women and a couple of men, Ruby learned, had been tried and even executed as witches for nothing more than talking in their sleep, making an unfortunate comment, or being in the wrong place at the wrong time. And this had happened right here in Camden Falls! Alice Kendall wasn't one of those people, since she was a made-up character. But the things that happened to her in the play were the sorts of things that happened to people accused of practising witchcraft in colonial Camden Falls. In the play, Alice Kendall is the neighbour of a man named John Parson, whose two young children have recently died of the flu. When Mr Parson's cow also dies, and he then recalls that one day he dropped and broke a china plate just as Alice was walking by his window, he begins to suspect that she's a witch.

His suspicions grow when he passes Alice in her garden one day and hears her talking to herself. John then notices a large crow, which he calls a "familiar", perched on the roof of the Kendalls' house. This is the beginning of Alice's troubles. Her family is shunned, and eventually Alice is executed after a supremely unfair trial, to Ruby's way of thinking. One witness says he saw a crow follow Alice Kendall across her garden. Another says that one day when her husband was ill, she asked to borrow some grain from the Kendalls. Alice Kendall said they had no grain to spare and the next day the woman's husband took a turn for the worse. These incidents are cited as further evidence of witchcraft.

Ruby's mind wandered as she lost herself in the world of seventeenth-century Camden Falls.

"Ruby?" said Ava. "Earth to Ruby."

Ruby blinked. "Sorry. I was thinking about Alice Kendall."

"Why would you want to play a witch?" asked Ava. "That's not a good character."

"Yes, it is. It's the best kind," said Ruby. "Alice was accused of something she didn't do. That's a great role for any actor."

"But in the end she dies."

"I know. I've always wanted to do a death scene."

Ruby sensed that if her sister could hear her, she wouldn't approve of what Ruby was saying. Not at all. Flora's mind was a complicated muddle of experiences and memories and thoughts that swirled around like the whirlpool above a drain. If Flora heard the words "death scene", her mind would immediately turn to the car accident and the death of their parents. But Ruby was able to put things in separate compartments in *her* mind. The death of her parents was sorted into one spot, the death of a fictional witch into another. And Ruby desperately wanted the chance to cough and gag and fall down onstage before an entire auditorium full of people.

The sound of clapping hands drew Ruby's and Ava's attention to the front of the room.

"Good morning," said Mr Lundy as he stood up from his desk. "Find your seats, please, people."

Ruby slid into her chair, stuffing several books and a small china crow into her desk as she did so. Ruby had a large collection of china animals at home and she had brought the crow to school that day for good luck. She knew that a crow had got Alice Kendall in trouble, but she felt *her* crow might be a good-luck charm.

Ruby was thinking how lucky she was to live in the twenty-first century, when it was OK to carry good-luck charms and to like crows without being accused of witchcraft, when she heard Mr Lundy say, "Ruby? Are you with us?"

Ruby straightened up. "Yes."

"Good. Because I was talking about the three

hundred and fiftieth birthday festivities, and I know they're of interest to you." (Ruby nodded.) "Now, as you know," Mr Lundy went on, "there are plenty of birthday events that you can participate in. The town will be holding an exhibit of art and another of photographs, and each will include work done by students at Camden Falls Elementary. Also, the auditions for the school play will be held this afternoon."

Ava raised her hand. "Ruby's going to try out for the part of the witch," she said, and Ruby smiled at her teacher.

"For the part of Alice Kendall?" asked Mr Lundy.

Ruby nodded. "I think I would make a very good witch," she said.

"I'm sure you'd do a fine job, but I'm not sure you'll be able to try out for specific roles," said Mr Lundy. "I think everyone will be asked to read a few lines, and small groups will be asked to perform scenes. Then the roles will be assigned. In other words, after the director has seen you, Ruby, she'll decide which role will be the best for you. Do you understand? You won't be able to try out just for the part of Alice Kendall. And remember, kids in all the grades will be trying out for the play. Sixth-graders, too."

Ruby knew what Mr Lundy was trying to say. It was just what Flora had said to her after the first day of school – that the starring role might go to an older kid, not a fourth-grader. But Ruby couldn't picture herself playing any part other than that of Alice Kendall, the poor, misunderstood, wrongly accused woman. So all Ruby said to Mr Lundy was, "OK."

The day of the tryouts, Ruby thought, was surely the longest since school had begun that year. She couldn't pay attention to much of anything Mr Lundy said, and by the afternoon she found herself seated in a chair right next to him – at his desk, facing the rest of the classroom. "Ruby," said Mr Lundy, "you're about two steps away from not being allowed to audition. *Please* pay attention."

Ruby did so. And when class was finally dismissed, Mr Lundy said to her, "Good luck, Ruby."

"Thank you!" Ruby shoved the china crow into her pocket and ran down the hall, as Ava and several other classmates called after her, "Good luck! We hope you get to be the witch!"

The tryouts were to be held in the auditorium. When Ruby arrived, she found Flora and Olivia waiting for her.

"What are you doing here?" she asked.

"We came to watch," said Flora.

"To cheer you on," added Olivia. "Are you nervous?"

"Nope."

"Ruby never gets nervous," said Flora.

"That's not true. *Sometimes* I get nervous."

"Hardly ever."

"Well, don't fight about it," said Olivia.

"People! People! May I have your attention, please?"

"That's Mrs Gillipetti," said Olivia. "I think she's going to be your director."

"Olivia and I will watch from back here," said Flora. "Good luck."

"Thanks." Ruby joined a crowd of kids that had gathered around Mrs Gillipetti in front of the stage. Many of the kids, she noted, were fifth- and sixth-graders.

"Good afternoon. I'm Mrs Gillipetti," said the director. "For those of you who don't know me, I teach fifth grade here, and I'm going to direct the play. Please sign in," she added, holding out a clipboard to be passed around. "Have you all read the script?"

"Yes!"

"I read it four times," Ruby called out.

"Wonderful," said Mrs Gillipetti. "Then you know that there are plenty of roles in the play. There's Alice Kendall, of course, and the people in her family; there's John Parson and his family; and there are all the people who participate in the trial, as well as other people who live in Camden Falls." She paused and took in the crowd of kids. "I'm sure there will be a part for everyone who is here. Some parts are big, some are small, some are nonspeaking roles, but each part is important to the play."

Ruby frowned. The part of Alice Kendall, she thought, is surely the most important of all, and much more important than some townsperson who doesn't even get to say anything.

Mrs Gillipetti picked up a stack of papers and handed them out to the kids. "These are some scenes from the play," she said. "You'll be reading them this afternoon. If any of you younger children can't read yet," she went on, looking at two tiny kindergartners, "your parents or older brothers or sisters may help you.

"Please take a few minutes to study the lines. Then I'll ask you to come up on the stage – sometimes one at a time, sometimes in groups – to read for me."

Ruby shot her hand in the air. "When will we find out what parts we've got?"

"Next Monday afternoon," replied Mrs Gillipetti.

Ruby swallowed. "OK." She felt for the crow in her pocket. Then she sat down in the first row of seats and studied the scenes. "Do we have to memorize the lines now," she asked Mrs Gillipetti, "or can we read from the pages?"

"You may read from the pages."

Ruby was pleased to see that one of the scenes was between Alice Kendall and John Parson. She whispered the lines as she read them and paid no attention whatsoever to the other kids in the auditorium. When she heard Mrs Gillipetti call her name, she ran on to the stage, pages in hand. "I'm ready," she said.

"OK. You'll be reading the first scene with me. Take the part of Alice and I'll be John."

Ruby drew in a deep breath, threw out her chest and read her lines at full volume. "So everyone in the back row can hear me," she informed Mrs Gillipetti. At the end of the scene, Ruby said, "Could I please act out the death scene for you? The one from the very end of the play?"

"But it isn't on the sheet," Mrs Gillipetti said. "And—"

"OK, then just watch me die." Ruby clutched at her chest with both hands. "Oh, ohhhhhh," she moaned. She coughed twice (delicately, so as not to overdo things), staggered and dropped to the stage. "See?" she said to Mrs Gillipetti. "It's understated but effective."

Mrs Gillipetti pursed her lips, and even from the back row of the auditorium, Flora could tell that she was trying not to smile. "Ruby," said Mrs Gillipetti, "answer me this: can you take direction? Because it's important to be a good actor, but it's just as important to be able to listen to your director."

Ruby stood up. "I can follow directions," she said seriously.

"OK, then. That's fine."

The audition ended two hours later, and Ruby ran to find Flora and Olivia. "Did you see me? Did you see me?" she asked breathlessly.

"You were hard to miss," said Flora, who then added, "but you did a really good job."

"Thank you. Oh, boy. How am I ever going to wait until Monday?"

Flora had a feeling it would be a long wait for anyone who knew Ruby.

10

Scary Mary's House

An autumn afternoon on Main Street, thought Flora, was a very nice thing. She poked along after school on the following Monday, pausing to look in windows and to call hello to the store owners. She was enjoying herself so much that she passed right by Needle and Thread, thinking that Min would hardly care if she was ten minutes late. Flora didn't often have an afternoon all to herself. But Ruby was at school, waiting to find out about the auditions for the play, Nikki had gone home to watch Mae, and Olivia was at her after-school Whiz Kidz class, making volcanoes and doing tricky maths puzzles that mystified Flora when Olivia later tried to teach them to her.

Flora sauntered into Ma Grand-mère and studied the array of pumpkin-shaped gingerbread cookies.

"How about a free sample?" asked Lisa, a new kid behind the counter.

"Sure!" said Flora. "Thanks."

She nibbled the cookie as she peered into the window of Time and Again a few minutes later, noting that a copy of *Understood Betsy* had been added to the display.

She poked her head into the post office and called hello to Jackie and Donna. And then, cookie finished, she made her way back to Needle and Thread.

"Howdy!" called Sonny Sutphin, who had parked his wheelchair in front of the store.

"Hi, Sonny." Flora wished she had another cookie so she could offer it to him. She remembered the first time she had met Sonny, just a few days after she and Ruby had moved to Camden Falls. Min had made introductions, and then Sonny had wheeled himself away down Main Street. Nothing more had been said about him. Once, weeks later, Flora had asked Min on a warm evening, "Does Sonny live by himself? He's almost always alone."

Min had replied, "Sonny is a very private person."

"But what's wrong with him?"

"Well, that's Sonny's business. It has to do with an accident, though."

Flora had sensed that she shouldn't ask further questions. And she hadn't.

Now she regarded Sonny solemnly and said, "They're giving away sample cookies at Ma Grand-mère."

Sonny smiled at her. "Thank you for the tip." He looked down at his twisted feet, then back at Flora. "Where are your cronies today?"

"My cronies?"

"Your buddies. Olivia and Ruby and the other girl."

"Nikki," Flora supplied. "They're all busy."

"You helping out in the store today?"

"Yup."

"OK, then. See you later. Say hi to your grandmother for me."

Flora waved at Sonny as he eased away in the direction of Ma Grand-mère, then let herself into Needle and Thread.

"There you are, sweetie," called Min. "How was school?"

"Fine."

"Good. Don't get too comfortable because I have a job for you."

"What is it?"

"I need you to take a package over to Mary's house."

"Mary's? Mary *Woolsey's*?" Flora's voice rose to a squeak.

"Yes, to Mary Woolsey's. It will be fine, Flora. And Gigi and I really need you to do this. It will save everyone a lot of time if Mary gets this fabric today."

Flora felt her heart begin to race and had a feeling she was blushing. She cast about for an excuse – homework, some urgent knitting project – but came up with nothing that couldn't wait until the evening. "Can't Mary come over here and get it herself?"

"She's working. She has a lot to do."

"Well," said Flora, but Min was already placing a package in her hands and ushering her out of the door.

"You know where Mary's house is, don't you?"

Flora gulped. She knew, all right. It had been one of the first things Olivia had shown her after Flora and Ruby had arrived in Camden Falls. And then Olivia had shared with Flora the tales about buried treasure in Mary's garden, a hapless child hidden in her basement. "Yes," said Flora, and before she knew it, she was stumbling down Main Street, Mary's package clutched in her sweaty hands.

How could Min do this to her? she thought. Make her go to Scary Mary Woolsey's. Alone. But she had no choice, and presently her feet were leading her to the little house that looked to Flora like a fairy dwelling. It was a different place in the autumn than it had been at the beginning of summer. When Flora had first seen it – the tiny house set among so many flower beds that it appeared to be an island rising out of an ocean of flowers – the garden had seemed alive with butterflies and insect noises and the sweet scent of blossoms. Now, on this chilly day, Mary's garden was a quieter place. Flora heard a few stray crickets, but that was all. She saw no butterflies, and the flowers that had been lush in June were now sparer, the colours muted and dull.

Flora paused for a moment at the end of the path that led to Mary's house, wondering briefly where, exactly, a treasure might be buried. Then she walked resolutely along the flagstones and climbed two stone steps. She raised her hand to ring the doorbell and saw that there wasn't one. Instead, there was an old-fashioned knocker in the shape of a lion's head on the door. Flora's mind flashed to the knocker on Scrooge's door in *A Christmas Carol*, the one that had shifted into the ghostly image of the long-dead Marley, and she shivered. She reached for the knocker, but before she could lift it, the door swung open.

There stood Mary Woolsey.

"Hi!" said Flora, her voice coming out as a croak.

"Is that Flora, then?" asked Mary. "Or Ruby?"

"It's me. I mean, I'm Flora."

Flora held out the package, but instead of taking it, Mary held the door open wider. Flora hesitated, then stepped inside. She listened for the sound of cries coming from the basement but heard only a clock ticking. And her own loud breathing.

I'm in Mary Woolsey's house, she said to herself. *Inside it*. If only Olivia could see me.

Mary closed the door behind Flora and stood watching her.

Flora held the package out further. "I brought the fabric," she said. "Min told me you need it today."

Mary ducked her head. "Yes. I do. Thank you." At last, she took the package.

Flora turned towards the door, but Mary didn't open it. "Well . . . your gardens are really nice," said Flora. "I saw them in the summer."

"They're not so much to look at now, I know."

"Oh, I didn't mean that!" cried Flora. "They're still really nice. I saw those flowers with the long name, the ones that smell good. I can't remember—"

"Chrysanthemums," said Mary. "A reliable autumn flower. If the deer don't get them."

Flora saw that Mary's hands were shaking and realized that Mary wasn't any more comfortable having a visitor in her house than Flora was being a visitor. Her eyes travelled to Mary's neck, and there was the star necklace. Flora opened her mouth to say "I guess I should go" and instead found herself saying, "I saw an old picture of you."

"What?" said Mary.

"In a box of stuff in Min's attic. And you were with my mother when she was a little girl. And you were wearing that same necklace," said Flora in a rush, pointing to the star. "And I was interested because it was my mother, and I didn't know you knew her, and my mother died." Flora put her hand over her mouth. What was she *say*ing?

But she found that Mary was looking at her softly.

"Sorry," said Flora.

Mary set the package on a chair by the door. "Nothing to be sorry about. Come, let's sit down." She turned and walked through a doorway, leaving Flora to follow her. "This is the parlour," she said tersely.

The parlour was a tidy room with a couch and

two armchairs covered in a faded blue-and-white fabric that Flora thought Min would call chintz. On the walls were exactly two pictures (both paintings of Mary's gardens) and a cuckoo clock that Flora hoped would chime while she was there. Several tables were crowded with framed photos, wooden boxes, small glass birds, snow globes and china teacups. Curled at one end of the couch were two orange cats whose slumber was not disturbed by the arrival of Flora and Mary. The room, Flora thought, was simple but cosy, and she felt at home in it.

Mary sat on the couch, and Flora was about to sit in one of the armchairs when instead she asked, "May I pat the cats?"

"Certainly," said Mary. "They probably won't even wake up. They're very old."

"What are their names?" Flora leaned over and stroked the cats' heads. One opened an eye, then closed it, and the other began to purr.

"Daphne and Delilah," Mary replied.

"We have a cat. His name is King Comma," said Flora, "because he has a white comma on his forehead."

"Ah, a fine name."

Flora sat in one of the chairs then, and Mary

regarded her for a moment before saying, "Tell me about this photo."

Flora described it to her. "Min said she wasn't sure, but she thought it was taken one day when you came over to her house. A long time ago. When my mother was four years old."

Mary frowned, then brightened. "My goodness. Is there a photo from that day?"

"Yes. You remember the day?"

"I do. It was the first time I was ever in your grandmother's house. I was looking for your great-grandfather."

"Min said you wanted to thank him for something."

Mary's gaze left Flora and travelled out of the window. "He had been very kind to me. I'd just found out about it."

Flora sat on the edge of the chair, hands clasped between her knees. She felt that if Mary didn't tell her what her great-grandfather had done, she would explode. Ruby or Olivia might have urged Mary on, but Flora couldn't. So she waited.

"That was such a time," Mary said finally. "My mother had just died—" Mary caught herself, her gaze jumping back to Flora. "Oh, I'm sorry."

"That's OK," murmured Flora, "really."

Mary cleared her throat. "My mother had just died," she said again. "Only I was much older than you. A grown woman. And I had been clearing some things out of the house. This house," she said. "I've lived here all my life. I came across some old letters and papers that had belonged to my mother, and suddenly I realized something. I realized that your great-grandfather must have been the one who'd been helping me out for years. With anonymous gifts of money." Mary paused. "Well, it's a long story," she said, "a very long story."

Flora nearly fell off the chair. She wanted to cry out "Don't stop now!" and might have done so if the cuckoo clock hadn't suddenly chimed. Flora jumped, then turned to look at the clock. She had read about cuckoo clocks in books but had never seen one, and she felt quite rewarded when a door on the front of the house-shaped clock opened and a painted wooden bird slid through it. Flora heard four distinct "cuckoos", then the bird retreated backwards through the door as if the house had sucked it inside.

"So," said Mary, "are you the one who likes to sew or the one who likes to sing and dance?"

Flora sighed. "The one who likes to sew. And knit and embroider and make cards."

Mary smiled. "My mother taught me to do those things. Well, not to make cards. But she taught me how to do all kinds of needlework."

"Min mostly taught me," said Flora. "My mother taught me a few things, too."

"And who taught your sister to sing and dance?"

"I don't know. I mean, no one. Ruby just does things. She's already in the chorus, and she's taking dance classes, and she tried out for the school play. She's going to find out today if she got a part."

"She's fitting right in here, isn't she?" asked Mary. And Flora looked up in surprise, remembering how she had thought of Ruby as a puzzle piece. When Flora said nothing, Mary went on. "But sometimes it takes a long time to fit in."

Later, Flora walked back to Main Street, thinking that there was probably not a whit of truth to the rumours about Mary Woolsey. Then she thought about what Mary had said about fitting in. She was still considering this when she entered Needle and Thread and was greeted by Ruby, who shouted, "Flora, I did it! I got the part of Alice Kendall! I'm going to star in the play!"

Nikki's Bad Day

Nikki Sherman was used to having bad days, but the bad day she had in the middle of October was supremely bad. Maybe it wasn't the worst one of her life, but it was right up there.

It hadn't started off badly. In fact, it had started off in the usual way for a Tuesday. She had called goodbye to her big brother, Tobias, when he was picked up by the bus that would take him to the high school. Then she and Mae, having already said goodbye to their mother (their father was sound asleep and couldn't be wakened, not that Nikki cared), climbed on to the bus to Camden Falls Elementary. The ride into town was almost pleasant (only two kids teased Nikki and Mae, and only one held his nose as they walked by), and when they got off the bus, Ruby and Olivia and Flora were waiting for them. Nikki was able to give her friends the news that after some carefully orchestrated conversations with her parents, she thought she and Mae had permission to go trick-or-treating.

"Except I want to be a princess," said Mae, "not that Toto dog."

Nikki and her friends walked Mae to her first-grade class as usual, Ruby chattering on about having got the lead in the witch play, and then Nikki and Olivia and Flora entered Mrs Mandel's room and took their seats.

After the morning business had been attended to, Mrs Mandel stood in front of her students, hands behind her back. That was when the regular day ended and the bad day began. Before Mrs Mandel had even opened her mouth, Nikki had a feeling she wasn't going to like whatever Mrs Mandel was going to say. And she was right.

"Class," their teacher began, "I have some news to share with you. My daughter is pregnant. My husband and I have known that for a while, and we're very happy."

Nikki glanced at Olivia, who was grinning, and she felt bad because she could tell by the look on Mrs Mandel's face that there was much more to her news, and that it was not going to be good.

"My daughter and son-in-law have been trying to have a baby for a long time," said Mrs Mandel, "and recently they learned that they're going to have triplets."

Olivia let out a whoop, then clapped her hand over her mouth, still grinning.

"My husband and I have been planning to move to the town where our daughter lives. We were going to do that next summer, which was one of the reasons I decided to retire.

"Now," continued Mrs Mandel, crossing her arms over her chest, which made her look stern when she didn't intend to look stern at all, "we've decided to move just after Thanksgiving so that we can settle in before the babies are born. We want to be able to help out as much as possible. That means" (Mrs Mandel paused and looked around the classroom) "that I'll be retiring at Thanksgiving."

Nikki's classroom was usually bustling and noisy. Now it fell quiet, as quiet as it had been on the rainy afternoon when Mrs Mandel read aloud from the most exciting part of *The Lion, the Witch, and the Wardrobe*.

After a few moments, Claudette Tisch raised her hand and said, almost in a whisper, "Does that mean you won't be our teacher any more?"

Mrs Mandel nodded. "When you come back to school after Thanksgiving, you'll have a new teacher. His name is Mr Donaldson. I've met him and spoken with him several times, and I think you'll like him very much."

Nikki glanced at Olivia again and saw that her grin had disappeared. Now she was looking at her desk, absently rubbing at a pencil mark with her forefinger. And Flora, Nikki thought, was trying not to cry.

"I'm sorry," said Mrs Mandel. "I know this is coming to you as a big surprise, but I'm doing what I feel is right. I want you to know, though, that I am going to miss every one of you very much. We've been together for just a few weeks but I can tell you're an extraordinary class. Mr Donaldson is going to be lucky to have you."

Olivia raised her hand and said quietly, "Maybe you could send us some pictures of the babies after they're born."

"And maybe," said Nikki, who rarely spoke up, "we could send you letters and things."

"That would be lovely," replied Mrs Mandel. "I'd be happy to send you pictures, and I'd be just as happy to hear from you."

Mrs Mandel smiled then, but Nikki wasn't able to

smile back. And for the rest of the day, even when she got a 100% on her spelling quiz, and even when she found that she had enough pocket money to buy an ice cream after lunch, she had the feeling that something was wrong.

Nikki couldn't escape the feeling. It was still hovering around her like fog when she returned home after school, and it only grew stronger when she discovered that her mother was in bed with a hangover. On the bus that afternoon, Nikki sat alone, since the first-graders had gone home at lunch time with the morning kindergartners while their teachers held a meeting. Nikki imagined telling her mother the news about Mrs Mandel. On her good days, Mrs Sherman was a patient listener with practical suggestions. But this was not one of those days.

Nikki stepped through the front door of her house to find Mae in the kitchen in the midst of a giant mess of crumbs, paper towels, spilled juice, smashed bananas and smears of peanut butter.

"Mae!" exclaimed Nikki, trying not to sound exasperated. "What – what is all this?"

"Mommy said I could fix my own lunch."

"Why didn't *she* fix it?"

"She's in bed. *You* know."

"Uh-oh," said Nikki. "And where's Dad? He's not

here, is he?" Mr Sherman would not tolerate Mae's mess.

Mae shrugged. "He wasn't here when I got home."

"OK." Nikki tiptoed upstairs to her parents' bedroom and peeked through the door, which was open several inches. Her mother lay slumbering on the bed, the sheets and blanket in a messy nest off to one side. Nikki tried to remember what her mother had been doing that morning when she and Mae left for school, and she realized she hadn't actually seen her mother, just spoken to her through the bathroom door. Nikki had been the one who made breakfast for herself and Mae and Tobias.

"Mom?" whispered Nikki, and when there was no answer, she closed the door quietly.

Back in the kitchen, Nikki looked at the clock on the oven. She didn't know where her father had gone, but if he had a job nearby, Nikki might have only an hour in which to clean up the mess and then feed Paw-Paw and the other dogs. The dogs were strays, all of them, and Nikki, who couldn't bear to see them starve, worked hard to be able to feed them. Her father, however, detested them. Nikki had to feed them in secret, had to save up her hard-earned money for weeks at a time in order to buy bags of chow, which she then kept hidden from her father.

"Have you seen Paw-Paw?" Nikki asked Mae.

Mae was sitting cross-legged in a kitchen chair, and Nikki noticed a smear of peanut butter on Mae's shin. "Mae, how on earth did you get peanut butter *there*?" she asked before Mae could answer her question about Paw-Paw.

"I don't know," said Mae. "It was hard to control."

Nikki couldn't help but smile. "The peanut butter?"

Mae nodded. Then she said, "Paw-Paw was sitting on the front steps when I got home."

Nikki dropped the sponge she'd been swiping across the table. "What? Are you sure? Right on the steps?"

Mae nodded again.

"Oh, no." This was not good, not good at all. The dogs – there were generally five to ten of them at any time – usually had the sense to hover around the Shermans' property, knowing Nikki would eventually feed them, but to stay out of sight when Nikki wasn't around. If Paw-Paw or any of the others had been sitting on the front steps and Mr Sherman had come home, well, who knew what might have happened. Mr Sherman screamed at the dogs, he threw things at them, and on occasion he struck or kicked them. They were filthy beasts, he said, and he couldn't understand why anyone would waste money feeding them when it was hard enough scraping together money to feed the Shermans.

But Nikki loved the dogs and so did Mae, especially Paw-Paw, who she had named and was the only dog who had stuck around for longer than a month. The others came and went, and Nikki couldn't keep track of them, but she tried to care for them all anyway.

"Mae, we have to get this mess cleaned up and feed the dogs before Dad gets home." Nikki looked at the clock again. "I'm not sure I'm going to have time to do both."

"Maybe," said Mae, "I could feed the dogs while you clean the kitchen."

"That's a nice offer," said Nikki, "but I don't know when Dad is going to come back, and if he saw you feeding them—" Nikki caught herself, then said, "Well, you wouldn't be able to hide those bags of chow fast enough. They're so heavy. No, help me here and then let's just hope there's enough time to feed the dogs."

"I'm sorry I made a mess," said Mae.

"That's OK. It wasn't your fault." Nikki glanced

towards the stairs, thinking of her sleeping mother, who should have been available to help Mae with her lunch. Then another thought occurred to her. She had better wake her mother before her father got home. If her mother was still in bed, that would present another problem. Nikki's stomach started to churn. How was she going to get everything done in time?

She would just have to hurry and focus on her tasks, that was all. Kitchen first, because the very last thing she wanted was for Mae to get in trouble. Then wake her mother. Then try to feed the dogs.

"OK, Mae. Let's get cracking," said Nikki, forcing her lips into a smile. "You put away the peanut butter and all the other things you took out of the cupboard. I'll wash the dishes, you dry them, and we'll both put them away. Is the Dustbuster working? There's a lot of crumbs and stuff on the floor."

"Broken," said Mae.

"Oh, well," said Nikki. "I'll use the broom."

Half an hour later, the kitchen looked fairly clean. "Let me go wake up Mom," said Nikki. "You stay here. Don't go outside yet."

"Um, Nikki? I think Dad's home."

Nikki had been halfway up the stairs. Now she

turned around, ran back to the kitchen, and peered out of the window. "Oh, no," she said under her breath. "Mae, go sit very, very quietly in front of the TV. Keep the sound low."

"But what about Paw-Paw?"

"There isn't time to feed the dogs. Just do what I say. I have to wake up Mom."

Nikki ran upstairs again and shook her mother. "Mom! Dad's home. You have to get up. You don't want him to know you slept all day. Get *up*."

To Nikki's relief, her mother rolled groggily out of bed and started to put on some clothes that were lying on a chair.

Downstairs the front door opened.

"Hi, Dad!" called Nikki cheerfully as she bounced down the steps.

"Hi, Daddy," said Mae cautiously from her seat on the couch.

"Where's your mother?" asked Mr Sherman.

"She'll be right down," replied Nikki.

"What's for dinner?"

"Mmm. . ." Nikki mentally reviewed the contents of the fridge and the freezer. "Hamburgers and peas."

Mr Sherman grunted, then dropped on to the couch.

"Mae, come on and help me start dinner," said Nikki.

Later, when Tobias returned from his after-school job, the entire Sherman family sat down to dinner, something that rarely happened. They arranged themselves around the kitchen table and ate in silence until Tobias cleared his throat and said, "So how's old Camden Falls Elementary, Nikki?"

"Good," said Nikki, who wasn't prepared to talk about Mrs Mandel's departure while her father was around.

"What about you, squirt?" Tobias asked Mae. "What do you think now that you're a big first-grader?"

Mae smiled. "It's fun. But sometimes it's cold on the playground. Mommy, is Mrs DuVane going to buy me a new coat?"

Mrs DuVane was a wealthy woman in Camden Falls who, because she had gone to high school with Mrs Sherman, had decided that Tobias, Nikki and Mae were her own personal charity projects. She frequently turned up (uninvited) to take them shopping for school clothes or supplies, or out for a meal in a fancy restaurant, or to a play or other cultural event.

At the mention of Mrs DuVane, Mr Sherman

snorted and said, "That old bat." Then he returned to his hamburger.

Tobias changed the subject. "Hey, Nikki, are you going to enter any of your pictures in the art show? The one for that town birthday thing? You should."

"I can answer that question," said Mr Sherman. He took a swallow of beer. "No, she isn't. We are Shermans and we don't need any attention drawn to us." He turned to Nikki. "You stay out of the spotlight, understand? Especially with any of that flaky art stuff. We are workers, not *artistes*." He waved his fork through the air, pinky raised.

Nikki nodded.

Mr Sherman turned to Tobias. "Get me another beer."

"You want another beer? OK." Tobias opened the refrigerator door, took out a cold can of beer and threw it at his father.

"Tobias!" cried his mother, and Mae screamed.

Mr Sherman ducked just in time, and the can crashed into the wall above the sink, leaving a mark in the greying paint. Tobias ran for the door.

"You get back here!" Mr Sherman was on his feet in a flash, but by the time he reached the door, Tobias had disappeared into the darkness. "He'd better not come home tonight," said Mr Sherman, who slammed the door so hard a picture fell off the wall. Then he took his place at the table again, leaving the beer can on the floor.

The Shermans finished their supper in silence, and that was the way Nikki's bad day ended.

12

Plans

The month of October became one of the busiest times in Camden Falls that Flora and Ruby could remember. Everyone seemed to be planning something or getting ready for something – making lists and phone calls, sewing, shopping and baking. Halloween costumes took shape. Rehearsals were scheduled. Meetings were held, some in secret.

At Min's house, Flora and Ruby and Nikki gathered to discuss the surprise party for Olivia's big one-oh. At school, Olivia and Nikki and Flora got the idea to give a hello/goodbye party for Mr Donaldson and Mrs Mandel, and to make presents for the triplets. At the Edwardses' house, Robby and his parents talked about what Robby might do after he graduated from school next spring.

The official planning for Olivia's party got under way in Flora's bedroom on a Saturday morning when Olivia and her brothers were spending the day with their grandparents.

"The main thing," said Flora, sitting at her desk with a pad of paper on her knee, "will be keeping this a secret from Olivia. Are we all going to be able to keep this huge secret?" Flora looked in Ruby's direction and raised her eyebrows.

"Why are you looking at *me*?" Ruby cried.

"At you? You mean at Ruby Jane Beanspiller?" said Flora.

Nikki giggled.

"It's not funny!" said Ruby.

"Yes, it is," said Nikki. "Ruby Jane Beanspiller?"

"That's what our parents started calling her almost as soon as she learned to talk," said Flora. "She blabbed everything to everyone."

Nikki's smile faded. She never knew what to say when the subject of Flora and Ruby's parents came up. Nikki didn't care much for her own father, but she couldn't imagine how she'd feel if both of her parents were taken away – *snap* – in a single unexpected moment.

"Well, *any*way," said Ruby, glaring fiercely at her sister, "I can keep this secret, and I think we have more important things to do. Like make plans. Where are we going to have the party?"

"Yeah, and how are we going to pull it off as a surprise?" asked Nikki.

"We should make lists," said Ruby. "For food, supplies, guests."

Flora held her pad of paper aloft. "That's why I have this."

"What about gifts?" asked Nikki.

"She wants a pet," said Flora.

"A pet? I – well, you know I don't have much money. How can we get her a pet?"

"I don't know. We'll have to talk to her mom and dad. I thought we could make most of her gifts anyway. We can get supplies at Needle and Thread. And look at all my craft stuff here. You can make cards – I've already made one for her – and some of the decorations, too. Olivia wants everything in silver and pink. I have lots of ideas. Now, here's what I think we should do. We should meet—"

Ruby interrupted her. "You sound like Olivia!" she said.

Flora smiled. "Do I?"

"Yeah," said Ruby. "It's nice. All bouncy like Olivia. Not sad."

"Well, anyway," said Flora, flushing and looking

down at the pad of paper, "I thought we could meet on the afternoons when Olivia's at Whiz Kidz."

"But I have rehearsals some of those days," said Ruby.

"And I don't know if I'll always be able to come into town," said Nikki. "Sometimes I have to go home after school. It kind of depends on ... things."

"What things?" asked Ruby.

"You know. My father. . ."

"What's wrong with him?"

"Ruby," said Flora, a warning in her voice.

"It's OK," said Nikki. "My father – he drinks. Mom, too. And sometimes my father has a job, sometimes he doesn't."

"What does he do?" asked Ruby. "I mean, when he has a job?"

"Lots of things. Carpentry, yard work, house painting."

Ruby was going to ask Nikki another question, but she glanced at Flora and saw her shake her head ever so slightly.

"So," said Flora, "we can *try* to meet on Olivia's Whiz Kidz days, and if we can't, well, maybe Ruby and I can just call you sometimes, Nikki, to see if you could come over."

"It would be better if you asked me at school," said Nikki, "because our phone doesn't always work." This was met with silence, so finally Nikki said brightly, "But look. Here we are together right now. Let's start making a list of guests first. Write down our names. And then write down. . ."

On this same Saturday, three doors down at the Row Houses, Robby and his parents sat around the kitchen table. Robby liked Saturday mornings very much, because often both of his parents were at home. They made a pot of coffee, something Robby liked to smell although not to taste. The coffee was poured into big brown mugs that Robby had bought his parents for Christmas the previous year. One mug said HIS on it and the other said HERS, and they had cost Robby more than sixteen dollars, but he had been happy to spend it on his parents.

"Robby," said his mother, setting the HERS mug on the table, "you know, we have something very important that we need to start thinking about."

"Christmas?" asked Robby.

His mother smiled. "Well, we probably should start thinking about Christmas, but I had something else in mind."

"Halloween?" Robby scowled.

"No. I was thinking about your graduation next year."

"When Margaret Malone graduates, she's going to have a party. She said so."

"That's a very nice idea," said Mr Edwards. "Would you like to have a party, Robby?"

Robby nodded. "For all my friends, like David and Bradley and Amanda from school. And Olivia and Margaret and Flora and Ruby." He paused. "Well, I don't want a party with all girls, though!"

"We'll get back to the party in a bit," said his mother. "What I was thinking about, Robby, is what you're going to do after you graduate."

"And after I have the party?"

"Yes."

"We've talked about your getting a job," said Mr Edwards. "But you know, you can stay in school for a few more years if you'd like."

"But I want to graduate with all the other people who will be eighteen," said Robby.

"I know. And you will. You can go to graduation. It's all set. But after that, you can continue with your schooling, just like most of the other students will."

"They'll go to college," said Robby. "Will I go to college?"

"No. But you can stay on with Mrs Fulton."

"In her class at the school for babies?"

"Robby," said his mother.

"But I don't want to stay there."

"That's fine. Then let's think about a job."

"A job! Yes! That's what I want to do. I want to work at Stuff 'n' Nonsense."

"With Mrs *Grindle*?" asked Mr Edwards. Mrs Grindle, the owner of Stuff 'n' Nonsense, took a dim view of children in her store and also considered Robby to be a child.

"I'm glad you've been thinking about this," said Mrs Edwards. "But what if Mrs Grindle doesn't have a job available? Is there anywhere else you'd like to work?"

Robby looked at the ceiling. "At Needle and Thread?" he suggested.

"So you want to work in a store," said his father.

"Yes." Robby paused. "I am very definite about that."

"Well, then, we'll talk to your teacher," said Mrs Edwards. "We want to make sure you understand how to make change and stock shelves, things like that. Maybe you can practise those things with Mrs Fulton this year."

"Yes," said Robby with a grin. "Practise stocking fragile items on shelves."

Mr Edwards filled his cup again, then said, "Robby, a few minutes ago, you made a face when you mentioned Halloween. Why was that?"

"Because Halloween is for babies and I'm not doing a baby thing like trick-or-treating."

"You don't have to go trick-or-treating."

"Of course not," said his mother. "Would you like to stay home and be the one who hands out the candy this year?"

"*I* could hand it out?" asked Robby.

"If you want to. Will you miss trick-or-treating?"

"Maybe. But I'm still not going."

"You could wear a costume when you hand out the candy," Mr Edwards pointed out. "Like Min and Gigi do at the store."

Robby remembered the day when he had sat outside with Olivia and Flora and their new friend, Nikki. "I could be the Wonderful Wizard of Oz," he said.

It was on the playground one chilly, grey day that Olivia, Nikki and Flora, huddled by the doorway, waiting to get back inside the warm school building, came up with the idea to give a party for Mrs Mandel.

"And for what's his name, the new teacher," said

Olivia. "A party to say goodbye to Mrs Mandel and hello to – to, um. . ."

"Mr Davidson?" said Flora.

"Mr Donaldson," replied Nikki. "That's a great idea!"

"We should tell all the other kids," said Olivia, "and they should talk to their parents. We're going to need our parents to help out. And we should invite them to the party, too."

"Parents or *guardians*," said Flora.

Nikki said nothing.

After a pause, Olivia said, "Well, what should we do at this party?"

"Maybe we could say nice things about Mrs Mandel," replied Nikki. "Like how much she's meant to us. But you only have to stand up and talk if you want to."

"If we do that, then we should probably say nice things to Mr Donaldson," added Flora. "Like how much we're looking forward to having him as our teacher. Even if we aren't. We don't want him to feel left out."

"Maybe we could make stuff for them," said Olivia. "We could write thank-you letters to Mrs Mandel and draw pictures or something for Mr Donaldson."

"Should we give them presents?" asked Flora. "I mean, besides the letters and pictures?"

"We could make presents!" exclaimed Nikki. "They could either be for Mrs Mandel *or* for the triplets."

"That's a great idea!" said Olivia.

"I'm going to start sewing right away," said Flora. "Min can help me. I'll plan three coordinating smocked outfits for the babies. Bubbles – one white, one green, one yellow. That way they can be for either boys or girls. Oh, this is going to be so much fun! I hope I'll have enough time. That's a lot of sewing."

"We *are* going to be awfully busy," said Olivia. "Which is good."

"Why is it good?" asked Nikki.

"Because it will take my mind off the big one-oh. It makes me too sad to think about that now."

Nikki and Flora exchanged small secret smiles. Then the bell rang and a hundred and twenty-two students made a run for the door, leaving the playground still and empty on that damp October day.

13

Olivia's Surprise

Busy, busy, busy. Ruby couldn't believe how busy she was. Camden Falls was much smaller than the town she and Flora used to live in. Their old town was more like a little city, really. And here was teeny Camden Falls, in which Ruby had lived for less than four months, and already she was taking dance classes, singing with the Children's Chorus (preparing for a concert to be given on Thanksgiving morning), going to rehearsals for the school play and trying to memorize her lines (she was the star of the play, so of course she had more lines than anybody else), helping to plan Olivia's surprise party, and trying to stay out of trouble and keep up with her schoolwork.

Despite the fact that Ruby was seated under the watchful eye of Mr Lundy in the very first row in her classroom, she had already had to stay after school twice. Once for talking in class, and once for concentrating so hard on drawing a picture of Alice Kendall that she hadn't realized Mr Lundy was standing behind her, watching the drawing take shape. Also, the majority of her grades so far had been C's. In fact, all C's except for one B and one D. Min wasn't pleased, and neither was Mr Lundy, who felt Ruby wasn't working up to her true potential and also had a slight attitude problem.

"If you want to stay in the chorus and the play," said Min, "you'll need to pull yourself up at school."

"OK," said Ruby vaguely, her thoughts on Olivia's party.

This conversation was held at Needle and Thread one afternoon when Ruby had no rehearsals scheduled.

"So I want you to sit down right here and start your homework," said Min.

"But Flora and Nikki and I are supposed to talk about plans for Olivia's party," Ruby protested. "And look, here they come now."

"Ruby needs to do her homework before she can join you," Min announced to Flora and Nikki as they dropped their school things on the couches.

"Really? But, Min, it's so hard to find time to work

on the party when Nikki's around and Olivia isn't," said Flora. "Can't Ruby help us for just a little while? Please? I promise that tonight we'll both sit at the kitchen table to do our homework. You can watch us. And you can check our homework when it's done. Please, please, please?"

"Please?" added Nikki.

Ruby made her saddest face.

Min looked at the ceiling briefly, as if for guidance, then said with a huge sigh, "Good gravy. All right. Ruby, you can work with the girls for one hour. Then you must start your homework."

"Thank you! Thank you, Min!" cried Ruby, and she threw her arms around Min's waist.

The girls gathered at the table at the back of the store.

"Ruby, you have to stay out of trouble," said Flora. "Really. I don't think Min will put up with much more."

"I don't do these things on purpose," said Ruby.

"Then you have to start thinking about what you do. You have to pay attention."

"You sound like Mr Lundy."

"I can't help it. Seriously, Ruby, you need to concentrate. On something other than your lines and your music."

Ruby sighed. If only she could memorize dates and facts as easily as, say, a new song. Just the other night, when she was supposed to be working on division problems, she had discovered that she knew the entire second verse to "The Lonely Goatherd" from *The Sound of Music*. It was Ruby's dream (one of her dreams, anyway) to play the part of Brigitta in *The Sound of Music*. Gretl was actually a better part, as far as Ruby was concerned, but Ruby thought she was too old to play Gretl. And it made her feel quite sad to think that at age nine she had already missed a great opportunity.

"Ruby?" said Flora. "Ruby? See, you're not paying attention *now*. I'm talking to you about paying attention and your mind is ... where is it?"

"With Gretl in *The Sound of Music*."

"Ahem," said Nikki. "Could we please get back to the party? I can't stay very long this afternoon."

"All right," replied Flora with one last glare in Ruby's direction. "Here's the big news. Yesterday when Mrs Walter came into the store I talked to her about a pet for Olivia."

"Ooh, what did she say? Did she think it was a good idea?" asked Nikki.

"Yup," said Flora, rolling a spool of thread across

the table. "But she said it has to be a small pet, not a dog or a cat."

"You mean like a hamster or something?" said Ruby.

"Yes. And what Mrs Walter thinks Olivia would most like is a guinea pig. So – and this is the great part – if we buy a guinea pig for Olivia, her parents will get the cage and other supplies. Then all Olivia will have to buy is its food."

"Excellent!" cried Ruby.

Nikki caught the spool of thread as it rolled by her, and she peered at it with great interest. "How much," she said, "do you think a guinea pig will cost?"

Flora glanced at her sister. "I'm not sure. But I don't think it will be very much. And Min might help us out. Also, Min promised to give us supplies from the store for making gifts and decorations. So we shouldn't have to pay for much stuff at all."

"OK," said Nikki, relaxing.

"So," said Flora, "the invitations have gone out." (Ruby had made the invitations on her computer.) "Let's just hope everyone can keep the party a secret."

"It's a good thing the party is going to be held

here," said Ruby, "because if we had it at our house, Olivia might get suspicious."

"It'll be easier to decorate here, too," added Flora. "Olivia doesn't come into the store as much as she did before school started."

"So what should we do today?" asked Nikki. "Work on decorations or on the presents we're going to make Olivia?"

"Presents, I think," said Flora. "They'll take more time. Do you guys know what you're going to make?"

"I do," said Nikki, "but I might need you to help me, Flora. I want to make Olivia a bag to carry all her school stuff in. I saw a really pretty one in the window of Flare last week when I was waiting for Tobias to pick me up, and I thought, 'I could make that.' But I do think I'll need a little help."

"What did the bag look like?" asked Flora.

"Sort of patchworky. But otherwise it was just a plain bag with a handle. It was the fabric that made it so special."

"Oh!" said Flora. "That's a great idea. You get a pattern for a simple tote bag, but you piece together different fabrics to make the sides. I could help you with that. We can take fabric from the scrap bin."

"Do you think there's any velvet in the scrap bin?"

asked Nikki. "That's one of the things that made the bag so fancy. Velvet."

"There is," replied Flora. "But velvet is hard to work with because of its nap. It makes it kind of slippery. You know what's much easier to work with and looks almost as nice? It's this kind of very fine corduroy. I think it's called featherwale. I'm not sure, but I know Min and Gigi have some. We could use that. Or velveteen."

"This is going to be fun," said Nikki.

"What about you?" Flora asked Ruby. "What are you going to make?"

"I was thinking of making her a beaded necklace and bracelet. But I might need some of your beads, Flora."

"OK."

"Thank you," said Ruby. "And what are you going to make?"

"Well, I've been planning this for a while now. I decided to make Olivia a wish pillow."

"What's a wish pillow?" asked Nikki.

"Something I made up." Flora reached for a pencil and began sketching on a piece of paper. "See, I'm going to divide a pillow into nine sections by sewing down rows of ribbon and rickrack. And then in each square I'll sew a button or something that's meaningful to Olivia. The pillow is going to be off-white, and the ribbons will be purple. I'm also going to put a purple satin ruffle around—"

"Oh! Oh!" cried Nikki. "I just thought of something. I'm sorry to interrupt you, Flora, but this is a really great idea."

"What? What is it?" asked Ruby.

"Well, I was thinking about the guinea pig. I mean, I was listening to you, Flora, I really was. But I was also thinking about the guinea pig, and how great it would be if Olivia could choose the exact one she wants."

"But it's supposed to be a surprise," said Flora.

"I know. And this is the great part. I thought, what if we go to the Cheshire Cat with Olivia one day after school? We'll say we just want to look around. And then I could stand in front of the guinea pig cage and say, 'Aren't these cute? If you guys could have one, which would it be?' And then we could each choose one, and that way we'd know which one Olivia wants."

"And we can ask Sharon to hold it for us until the day of the party!" exclaimed Flora.

"Who's Sharon?" asked Nikki.

"She owns the Cheshire Cat. I know she'll do this for Olivia."

"Maybe we can go tomorrow," said Ruby.

"I'll call Olivia tonight," said Flora.

Then, with the guinea pig plan taken care of, the girls got down to the business of making Olivia's birthday presents.

When school let out the next afternoon, Flora, Olivia and Nikki met up with Ruby, who said casually, "I don't have any rehearsals this afternoon. Let's go walk around town. Can you come, Nikki?"

"Sure. And you know what? I've always wanted to look in the Cheshire Cat, but I never have."

"Well, let's go there," replied Flora. "OK, Olivia?"

"OK. I love the Cheshire Cat."

"Goody," said Flora, who had stopped in the pet store the day before and told Sharon their plan.

Olivia, Nikki, Flora and Ruby jostled one another and giggled on the short walk from Camden Falls Elementary to Main Street. They ran into Needle and Thread and stayed long enough to greet Min and Gigi and to dump their school bags behind the counter. Then they left for the Cheshire Cat – Nikki, Ruby and Flora exchanging meaningful smiles and pleased glances, hoping Olivia wouldn't notice anything unusual.

The Cheshire Cat, which sold pet supplies and small animals such as fish and birds and hamsters and mice but not cats or dogs ("Because there are plenty of cats and dogs in shelters who need homes," said Sharon), was located across Main Street and a few stores down from Needle and Thread.

"Let's look at the guinea pigs first!" cried Ruby as the girls charged through the door.

Nikki elbowed her. "You'll give it away!" she said in a loud whisper.

But Olivia was already standing in front of the guinea pig cage and exclaiming, "Ooh, they are cute. They are so, so cute. I wish, I wish, I wish I could have one of my own. See how fuzzy they are?"

"If you *could* have one, which would it be?" asked Nikki, crouching next to Olivia for a better look in the cage. "I like that brown-and-white one."

"Mmm, I like *that* one," said Olivia, pointing.

"The all tan one?"

"Yup. And I know what I would name it, too. Sandy. Isn't that a good name for a tan guinea pig?"

"It's perfect," said Flora.

The girls wandered around the store then and looked at all the animals and toys and treats and supplies. Before they left, Olivia returned to the guinea pig cage and took one long last look at Sandy. Then she opened the door to the Cheshire Cat and headed outside, followed by Ruby and Nikki. She didn't notice that Flora hung back just long enough to whisper to Sharon, "The all tan one, the one in the corner." Sharon nodded and said, "He's all yours. I won't let anyone else buy him."

Flora grinned and ran outside to join her friends.

14

Trick or Treat

"Happy Halloween! Happy Halloween!"

On the last day of October, a morning that dawned chilly and grey and gloomy, Flora was awakened by Ruby, who was bouncing on her bed, crying, "Happy Halloween!" She was already dressed in her costume.

"Ruby?" Flora rubbed her eyes and yawned widely. "What time is it?"

"Six-oh-five."

Flora groaned. "Ruby."

"What?"

"It's too early, that's what. We don't have to get up yet."

"But aren't you excited? It's Halloween."

Flora considered this. Was she excited? She was pleased with her costume and pleased with the other costumes she and Min had helped make. Alyssa's candle costume, for instance. And she was looking forward to the party in Mrs Mandel's room that afternoon. But she couldn't help remembering past Halloweens, and all of them involved her parents, especially her father, who had enjoyed Halloween even more than Flora and Ruby had. The costumes he had made for himself to wear as he handed out candy had been the talk of the neighbourhood, particularly since Mr Northrop had kept each costume a secret until Halloween. No one, not even Flora's mother, had known what the costume would be until he put it on in time to greet the first of the trick-or-treaters.

But this year will be different, Flora told herself. No one would be handing out candy from Min's house, and although she and Ruby would start their trick-or-treating at the Row Houses, they would finish up in town, going from store to store. And they would spend the evening with Olivia and Nikki instead of Annika and Liza and Ruby's friend Polly.

"Well, aren't you?" asked Ruby again.

Flora sat up and looked at her scarecrow costume, which was draped over the armchair in the corner of her room.

"Yes," she said. "I'm excited."

*

Although Min worried that the day was too chilly for trick-or-treating, Ruby said, "But it's perfect Halloween weather. It's all windy and grey. Kind of spooky."

By late in the afternoon, when Ruby and Flora and Olivia were putting on their costumes at the Walters' house, the day had grown even windier. And darkness had fallen early.

"It's like you could almost expect to see a real ghost," said Ruby, shivering as she peered out of the window. "Or a witch."

"Don't scare me!" exclaimed Olivia.

"Come on, you guys. Put on your costumes," said Flora.

"I need help," said Olivia, who was the Tin Man and had the most complicated of the costumes. She and Flora and Min and Mrs Walter had worked hard to create a silvery costume, complete with a funnel for a hat. "Where's the silver make-up? We have to cover my face with it."

Flora's scarecrow costume was the next most complicated, since she wanted real straw to show at her wrists and ankles and neck. Nikki, as the Cowardly Lion, would be wearing a brown bodysuit and a hood with a mane attached. Ruby was to be Dorothy.

"If I can't play Dorothy onstage, then at least I can dress like her," Ruby had said.

"Is everybody ready?" asked Mrs Walter, poking her head into the kitchen.

"Almost. But don't let the boys in here. Ruby's in her underwear," said Olivia.

"The boys have already left," replied her mother. She helped Ruby put on her dress and checked pinafore. "Wow," she said, stepping back. "You girls did a fabulous job. You look as if you could have stepped right out of the book. Where are you going to meet Nikki?"

"In town," said Olivia. "We're going to trick-or-treat on the way and then meet Nikki at . . . where did we say we would meet her?" she asked Flora.

"We didn't. We just said we'd find her somewhere. Nikki didn't know what time Tobias would be able to drive her and Mae into town."

"Well, have fun," said Mrs Walter. "Oh – let me take a picture of you before you leave. I wish I could get one with Nikki, but you three look pretty fantastic."

The picture she took, which Flora still has – stuck on the corner of the mirror in her bedroom – shows a grinning Scarecrow, a grinning Tin Man, and a grinning Dorothy, their arms thrown around one another.

"OK. Come on!" said Olivia. "I always start at Mr Pennington's because he gives out regular-size candy bars."

Laughing, Flora and Ruby and Olivia ran outside and into the Camden Falls night-time.

"Well, I'll be," said Mr Pennington a moment later when he answered his doorbell. "It's Dorothy Gale, the Tin Man, and the Scarecrow. What wonderful costumes."

"Thank you," said Olivia and Flora.

"Trick-or-treat!" said Ruby.

Mr Pennington did indeed have full-size candy bars, an entire bowl of Three Musketeers. "Now, be sure to go next door to the Edwardses' house. Robby's handing out the candy this year," he said.

"Oh, we will," said Ruby. "We have to see the Wizard."

When Robby opened his door, Olivia said, "Hello, Wizard of Oz. It's me, the Tin Man. I've come to see if you can give me a heart."

Robby smiled. "No, but you can have a Baby Ruth."

"I need a brain," said Flora.

Ruby eyed the Wizard's case, which Robby had perched on a bench in the hallway, and said, "Oh, I don't think there's anything in that black bag for me."

"Ha! That's a good one, Ruby! Just like in the movie."

"Are you *sure* you don't want to come trick-or-treating with us?" asked Olivia.

Robby looked away from the girls. "Nope. I mean, no, thank you. Thank you very much. I have a job. I'm an adult."

"OK, but we're going to miss you."

"You're an excellent Wizard," added Flora.

"Thank you," said Robby again.

The girls made their way to the rest of the Row Houses – except for Min's, of course – and then started for town. All along Aiken Avenue they passed groups of costumed trick-or-treaters, their wigs and capes and jackets and masks blowing in the wind. Some carried torches, some shouted. A few of the smallest children rode on their parents' shoulders. As the girls turned the corner on to Main Street, the wind shoved the clouds away, and for an instant Flora glimpsed the Halloween moon.

Ruby exclaimed, "I just saw a witch ride across

the moon. I swear I did! I saw her silhouette, and she was in flowing robes on a broomstick!"

Despite herself, Flora shuddered and looked once more at the moon, which was perfectly round and yellow but showed no signs of its path having been crossed by a witch.

"Wow!" said Ruby, her attention now drawn to Main Street. "Look at town. It's . . . it's enchanting."

Every store on Main Street was outlined in soft orange and gold lights. The windows were decorated with goblins and monsters and black cats and brooms and pumpkins and candy corn and cornstalks. The girls had already seen this, of course – town had been decorated for days – but now walking up and down the pavements were crowds of trick-or-treaters. And standing in the doorways of the shops were queens and magicians and cows and pirates and mummies, all waiting to hand out candy.

In the doorway of Needle and Thread were the Wicked Witch of the West and Glinda, each holding a plastic pumpkin full of candy.

"Hi, Min! Hi, Gigi!" called Flora and Ruby and Olivia.

"Hi, girls." Gigi turned to the Northrops. "How's your first Halloween in Camden Falls?"

"Great," said Flora.

"We have to find Nikki," said Olivia. "Have you seen her?"

"The Cowardly Lion?" asked Gigi. "Not yet."

So Olivia and Ruby and Flora set off down Main Street. They stopped in store after store, and their bags of candy grew heavier and heavier, but they didn't find Nikki.

"We should have had a better plan," said Olivia.

"I bet she and Mae are around here somewhere and we just haven't found them because it's so crowded," said Ruby.

"What time is it?" asked Olivia.

"Seven-thirty," said Flora.

By eight-thirty, the girls were tired, their bags were full, and they still hadn't found Nikki.

"Let's go to Needle and Thread," said Flora. "If Nikki's here, she'd look for us at the store."

In the little house at the end of the gravel driveway, kilometres away from Main Street, Nikki Sherman lay on her bed fully clothed. Her lion costume hung in the closet. In the bed next to her, Mae slept soundly in her princess costume. Nikki stood and tiptoed to the closed door of their room. She put her ear to the door, but very quickly she jumped back. She didn't have to listen hard to hear the voices from the kitchen.

"You said they could go!" That was her mother's voice, and Nikki sensed tears in it.

"Well, I changed my mind." That was her father.

"But it isn't fair. The kids had their hearts set on it. They have little enough as it is—"

Mrs Sherman abruptly stopped speaking and Nikki knew why. She winced.

"Little enough? You think I give my kids *little* enough?" Her father's voice rolled like thunder up the stairs to Nikki.

"That's not what I meant. It's just that—"

Nikki didn't need to hear the rest of the conversation. She tiptoed back to her bed and crawled under the covers.

On Aiken Avenue, the trick-or-treaters began to drift home. At several of the Row Houses, porch lights had been extinguished, indicating that all the candy had been given out. Min walked Ruby, Flora and Olivia home from Needle and Thread. "Goodbye!" they called to one another. Flora and Ruby ran to the living room to dump out their candy, sort it, count it and trade it. All the while, Flora wondered if she should phone Nikki, but in the end, she decided not to.

In the second Row House from the left, Mr Willet had already put his wife to bed. He hoped this would be one of the nights she stayed in bed. She'd been disturbed by the evening's trick-or-treaters, and Mr Willet didn't want her wandering downstairs, checking to see if the drapes were drawn against intruders He didn't have the energy to keep returning her to their room.

In the house on the north end of the row, Mrs Fong rubbed her hand across her swelling belly and said to her husband, "Next year I'll be able to make a costume for our baby. A pumpkin, I think. Or maybe a bumblebee."

Mr Pennington had run out of candy. He had turned out his lights, and now he and Jacques were settling into bed, Jacques's snout turned towards Mr Pennington so that he could feel warm doggy breath on his neck.

Robby Edwards was calling to his parents, "The candy is all gone! It's all gone! I think Halloween is over!"

"You did a great job," his father told him. "How did you like handing out the candy?"

"Fine. Yup, fine. When can we get our Christmas tree?"

And at Min's house, Flora breathed a sigh of

relief as she put her costume away in the wardrobe. She and Ruby had survived their first holiday without their parents. Before Flora turned out her light that night, she set two photos on her bedside table, one of her mother and one of her father, so that they were the last faces she saw before she fell asleep.

15

Happy Birthday, Olivia!

With Halloween behind her, Olivia turned her thoughts to her big one-oh. It would take place in just four days. And they were a busy four days, which was good, since the hustle and bustle kept Olivia's mind off the fact that after everything – after nearly ten years of a life well lived – her special day was not to be marked by the party for which she had longed.

On the day after Halloween, Olivia, Flora and Ruby walked to Camden Falls Elementary together as usual.

"Do you think Nikki will be in school today?" asked Ruby.

"She hasn't missed a day yet," replied Olivia.

"I know, but. . ."

Ruby didn't need to finish her sentence. The girls

were thinking the same thing and were equally worried.

They arrived at school the moment Nikki's bus did, and not long after it had wheezed to a stop and the door had opened, Mae hopped down the steps followed by Nikki.

"Nikki!" Olivia cried, and she rushed to hug her friend.

"What happened to you?" Flora asked, and she knew she sounded both relieved and exasperated, the way her mother had sounded years ago when Flora, then six years old, had wandered away at a playground, and her mother had had to call and call before she found her.

Nikki cast her eyes towards Mae and said lightly, "Hey, we don't want to be late. We can talk later on the playground."

So it was at recess that the story came out.

"He wouldn't let us leave the house, any of us," said Nikki as she and Olivia and Flora sat on the swings at the furthest edge of the playground.

"Why not?" asked Olivia.

Nikki shrugged.

"I don't understand," said Flora.

"Well, I don't, either," said Nikki. "Or maybe I do. Mom says my father sometimes just 'takes a notion'.

But what I think is that he likes to feel he can control us. He can't control a lot of other stuff, like whether he has a job or earns enough money, but he can tell Mom and Tobias and Mae and me what to do. You know what, though? He isn't going to be able to control Tobias much longer. Tobias stands up to him now."

Olivia stared across the playground. "We missed you last night," she said.

"I really wanted to come."

"Maybe someday he'll change."

"I don't see how that's going to happen," replied Nikki, and that was all she would say about her father and Halloween.

Wednesday, Thursday and Friday were busy with homework and a Whiz Kidz event and working at Needle and Thread and plans for Mrs Mandel's party. Before Olivia knew it, Saturday had arrived. Her big one-oh.

"Hi, everybody," said Olivia as she walked sleepily into the kitchen that morning.

There were her parents and her brothers, already up and already busy. Her parents were cooking breakfast, and her brothers were setting the table. Olivia saw paper plates and cups decorated with rainbows at each place and a bunch of balloons over the table.

"Surprise!" shouted Jack.

"Happy birthday!" said Henry and her parents.

"I bet you didn't expect a birthday breakfast, did you?" asked her mother.

Olivia smiled. It wasn't the one-oh bash she'd dreamed of, but it was nice.

"Open your presents, open your presents!" cried Jack.

"Right now?" asked Olivia.

"Yes! I can't wait."

Jack liked presents – his own, other people's. It didn't matter.

So while Olivia's parents finished making breakfast, Olivia tackled the little stack of presents on the floor next to her chair. She opened a paperback book and a CD and a kit for knitting her first scarf.

"Now open mine!" said Henry, holding out a sloppily wrapped package, which looked suspiciously like another CD.

Olivia had just pulled the ribbon off when the phone rang.

"I'll bet that's for you, sweetie," said her father.

Olivia picked up the phone. "Hello?"

"Happy birthday! Happy birthday! It's us. Flora—"

"And Ruby!"

"Are you having a good birthday so far?" asked Flora.

"Great," replied Olivia.

"Well, I just wanted to say that we won't be around today. Ruby has a special play rehearsal. Something about costumes. And I have to be there because I'm going to help with her costume."

"So you won't even be at the store today?" said Olivia.

"Nope. But we'll see you tonight. Or maybe tomorrow, OK?"

"OK." Olivia hung up the phone, feeling tears somewhere behind her eyes. "Flora and Ruby are busy," she said. "I thought . . . I don't know."

"Well, that's OK," said Mrs Walter. "We'll do something special. Maybe we'll go out to lunch."

At three o'clock that afternoon, after Olivia had indeed gone out for a special lunch – just Olivia and her mother, a girls' lunch – and she had opened some cards and two packages that arrived in the mail, the phone rang again.

"I'll bet it's for you!" said her father, who had said that every time the phone rang that day.

"Hello?" said Olivia.

"Hi, honey," said Gigi's voice. "Happy birthday!"

"Thank you."

"Listen, I was wondering if you could come to the store. Some fabric just came in for your mother, and I know she wants it. Anyway, I want to see my granddaughter on her birthday."

"All right," said Olivia, without any enthusiasm. "I'll see you in a few minutes." Olivia put on her hat and coat, called goodbye to her parents and set out for Needle and Thread.

She walked slowly down Aiken Avenue, noticing that most of the trees were now entirely bare and that the grass was turning from green to brown to yellow. Winter would arrive soon, she thought. A long, cold Camden Falls winter. She wondered if, by the time spring arrived, her father would have a new job. Or maybe her mother would have a job. Someone in her family needed to work.

Olivia turned the corner on to Main Street, scuffed through the last of the fallen leaves to the door of Needle and Thread, opened it, heard the familiar jangle of the bell and called out, "Hi, Gigi," even though she didn't see her grandmother.

"SURPRISE!"

The chorus of voices was so loud and so unexpected that Olivia jumped and stumbled backwards, causing the bell over the door to jangle again. From behind the couches, the checkout counter, bolts of fabric, and racks of notions, from under and in every possible hiding place in Needle and Thread jumped Olivia's friends and relatives. The store that had looked empty a few moments before was now crowded. There were Flora, Ruby, Nikki, Gigi and Poppy, Min, Mr Pennington, Olivia's other grandparents, Robby and his parents, the Fongs, every single Morris, Dr Malone and Lydia and Margaret, several of Olivia's classmates, two of her cousins, and her aunt and uncle.

"Are you surprised?" cried Robby. "Are you, Olivia? We tricked you!" He set a sequinned tiara on her head. "Here's your birthday crown," he added. Then he leaned over and whispered in her ear, "I kept a secret from you for a *very* long time. And it wasn't easy."

"I – I—" Olivia was nearly speechless. She started to sink down on one of the couches, but suddenly she was surrounded by Nikki, Ruby and Flora, who threw their arms around her.

"We've been planning this for ever!" exclaimed Flora.

"Notice how I did not spill the beans," Ruby whispered to her sister.

"Your parents were in on it, too, Olivia," said Nikki.

And at that moment, the bell jangled once again as Henry and Jack and Mr and Mrs Walter ran in.

"Surprise!" they shouted.

"What?" said Olivia. "How did—"

"We were waiting for Gigi's phone call," said her father. "We left the house right after you did and followed you here."

"You sure are a pokey walker," added Henry.

"Did we *really* surprise you?" Ruby asked Olivia.

"I'll say."

"Really and truly? You didn't suspect anything?"

"Not a thing. I can't believe this!"

"Look around the store," said Nikki. "We made all the decorations."

Olivia walked slowly around the store while her guests laughed and chatted. Taped to the walls were giant pink-and-silver insects made from cardboard and felt, with wire antennae and pipe cleaner legs. Spread across the coffee table was a white cloth, and Olivia could see that the guests had signed it and drawn pictures on it.

"Look over there," said Flora. "Gigi helped us with that."

"It's the Olivia Walter Timeline," added Ruby.

Propped up on the cutting table was a long piece of poster board marked off into years and noted with important events in Olivia's life. Under the timeline were ten photos of Olivia, one for each year, starting with the day she had been born, and with space for an eleventh photo.

"I can't believe it. I really can't believe it," Olivia said over and over again.

"And the party hasn't even started," said Flora. "You have to open your presents" (she pointed to the mountain of gifts teetering on one of the couches) "and we have to have the cake, of course."

"But before that," said Ruby, "we have an extra-special surprise."

"*Another* surprise?" said Olivia.

Ruby grinned. "Who wants to bring him out?" she asked.

The guests had gathered around Flora, Ruby, Nikki and Olivia, and Nikki said, "I'll get him."

"Him?" said Olivia.

Nikki disappeared into the storage room and emerged holding a box. It was a cardboard box that had been wrapped in pink-and-silver paper, the bottom separately from the top so that the lid could be lifted off. Nikki handed it to Olivia, and Olivia saw that holes had been poked in the lid.

"Open it carefully," said Nikki.

Olivia sat on a couch, the box in her lap. She raised the lid. Peering up at her were two bright black eyes. Olivia's mouth dropped open. "It's – is it . . . Sandy?" she asked.

"Yup," said Flora. "He's all yours."

"This is yours, too," spoke up Mr Walter, and he and Mrs Walter and Henry and Jack placed a guinea pig cage, a bag of litter, and a supply of food at Olivia's feet.

Olivia, the centre of attention, sat among her family and her three best friends, her new pet in her lap. "I can't believe it," she said once more, and then she added, "This is the best one-oh ever."

16

Paw-Paw

Nikki and Mae Sherman stood hand in hand outside the storage shed in which Nikki kept the bags of kibble for the stray dogs. Darkness was falling, but in the dim light they could just see the outlines of the other buildings on their property, fuzzy-edged shapes in shades of grey.

"I can't see the dogs, though," Mae was saying. "It's too dark."

"You can see their eyes," Nikki replied. "You can see their eyes shining in the light from the house. Count the pairs of eyes, Mae. I want to know how many dogs are coming for food now."

"More," said Mae with certainty. "It's more."

"I know. But I want to know how many more. You count and I'll count – we'll count to ourselves – and let's see if we come up with the same number."

Nikki scanned the edges of the property. A few minutes earlier, after she had hauled a bag of food out of the shed, the sound of kibble rattling into plastic bowls had called to the shining eyes, and they had appeared from all directions. Nikki started at her left and began to count. "One, two, three, four, five, six. . ." She reached nine and realized she wasn't done.

"Thirteen," said Mae a few moments later.

"I got twelve, but it's hard to see. Anyway, there are definitely more." Nikki let out her breath. "Wow."

"I thought you *wanted* to feed the dogs," said Mae.

"Oh, I do. It's just that there are so many of them now."

"But isn't that good? You're helping lots and lots of dogs."

"I guess so."

"They're all so skinny. Even Paw-Paw," said Mae. "They really need the food."

"I know." Nikki thought of her dwindling funds. It wasn't easy for her to find ways to earn money. She lived too far out in the country to have a regular job in town, and anyway, she was too young to be hired for most jobs. Every now and then, her mother paid her to babysit for Mae, but mostly her mother didn't have any money of her own. Tobias sometimes offered to pay Nikki for helping him with one of his projects – repainting a car or fixing an engine – but Nikki knew he was only creating work for her; he could just as easily do those things on his own. The Shaws down the road were her main source of income. She often helped them with farm chores. Still, the bags of dog food were expensive, and Nikki could only afford to buy so many.

"What are you doing?"

A voice spoke loudly from the darkness, and Nikki and Mae jumped, Mae grabbing for Nikki's hand as Nikki tried to shove the dog food and dishes under a bush.

"Relax, it's just me."

"Tobias!" scolded Nikki. "You scared us to death."

"We thought you were *Dad*," said Mae, and she ran fiercely towards Tobias and punched his leg.

"Ow!" exclaimed Tobias. "Mae, quit it. I didn't mean to scare you." He picked up his sister and held her at arm's length, giving her a warning look, then hugged her.

"Sorry," muttered Mae.

Tobias watched Nikki pull the dishes out from

under the bushes. "How many dishes *are* there?" he asked, his expression turning to surprise. "Seriously, Nikki, what's going on here?"

Nikki sighed. "Mae and I just tried to count the dogs. There are twelve or thirteen coming around for food now."

Tobias set Mae on the ground. He rubbed his forehead. "You know, the more dogs you feed, the more will come."

"I guess. I didn't realize that would happen. And I don't have enough money for all the food."

"Why don't you just put out less food?" asked Tobias. "This is nice, but it isn't really your responsibility. Besides, Dad hates the dogs, and he knows what you're doing, Nikki. Maybe he doesn't know how you get the food or where you hide it, but he knows you're feeding the dogs somehow, and it makes him angry."

"Well, I don't care. Let him be angry. That's his problem," said Nikki. "I'm not doing anything wrong. I'm doing a good thing. Besides, he's not the boss of me."

"I know. I agree. Just telling you," replied Tobias.

Two days later, on a warm afternoon that felt more like September than November, Nikki and Mae sat on the bare earth outside the shed in which the dog food was hidden. Nikki's solution to her problem – a temporary one, she knew – had been to set out three fewer dishes than before, to fill the other dishes only partway, and to feed the dogs earlier than usual, before her father was due home.

". . . eight, nine, ten!" said Mae, counting with great authority. "See? Not so many dogs as before."

"Yeah, but what happened to the others?" asked Nikki. "It doesn't mean they aren't hungry. It just means they know they can't get food here any more."

The hum of wheels could be heard on the county road, and Nikki and Mae paused in their conversation to listen. When the wheels slowed, Mae said, "That's Tobias! Tobias is home!"

Sure enough, the wheels began to crunch along the gravel driveway, and Mae jumped up. She ran towards the car, then turned around and dashed back to Nikki.

"It isn't Tobias! It's Dad!" she cried.

Nikki felt her stomach roll. What was her father doing home early? "Quick! Get the dishes while I put the food away." Nikki reached for the bag, which was a new one and mostly full. It weighed nearly ten kilos. She began to drag it towards the shed.

"The dogs are still eating!" said Mae. "I can't take the dishes away from them. They'll bite me."

But Mr Sherman slammed the door of his truck then, and most of the dogs bolted, disappearing from view. Paw-Paw and two others remained behind, though, stealing last bites from the dishes, even as their hackles rose and low growls rumbled in their throats.

Nikki had just reached the shed door and was preparing to heave the bag of food inside when her father stumbled towards Mae, a rake raised above his head.

"Mae!" shrieked Nikki, and she dropped the bag.

"What did I tell you about feeding these dogs, these filthy beasts, these mutts, what did I tell you?" Mr Sherman spoke deliberately and slurrily, spitting when he said the word "beasts". Then, stumbling, he pitched the rake in the direction of Paw-Paw and the last two dogs, who had finally abandoned the dishes and were slinking towards the edge of the property. Nikki heard a yelp when the rake landed in the underbrush.

Mr Sherman teetered across the yard, collected the rake, and approached his daughters again. They stood as if frozen until he raised the rake again and began to swing it downward. Then Nikki sprang forward, grabbed Mae and shoved her into the shed.

"You don't listen to me, you don't listen to me, any of you, what did I tell you, what did I tell you a thousand times?" said Mr Sherman in a frighteningly quiet voice.

"Not to feed the dogs?" whispered Nikki.

The rake crashed to the ground.

"Not to feed the dogs?" mimicked her father.

Nikki heard the front door to her house fly open then, heard it open with such force that it crashed against the wall. (Years later, Nikki would still be able to see the dent it left in the siding.) The next thing she knew, her mother was running across the yard. "Howie!" she yelled. "What is going on out here?"

"These two," said Mr Sherman, and Nikki had the unsettling notion that her father couldn't recall her name or Mae's at that moment, "these two have disobeyed my orders." He stopped to catch his breath. "Time and again," he went on, "time and again they disobey my orders."

Mrs Sherman caught her husband by the elbow. "Calm down," she said. "Just calm down. Leave the girls alone. Are you all right, girls?" she called over her shoulder as she led Mr Sherman towards the house.

Nikki, on the verge of tears but not wanting Mae to notice, nodded in answer to her mother's question, then realized that her mother couldn't see this, so she managed to croak, "Yeah." She waited until her parents had entered the house and her mother had closed the front door behind them before she led Mae out of the shed and knelt in front of her.

Mae sank down until she was sitting cross-legged on the ground. She rested her head in her hands and began to sob.

"It's OK, Mae," said Nikki. "He's inside. Mom took him inside."

Mae didn't answer, but her sobs grew quieter. Nikki put her arm around her sister.

"I was scared," said Mae.

"So was I. But this is what you have to think: nothing happened. He didn't hurt us and Mom came outside in time. So it's OK."

Mae jerked her head out of her hands then and stared off into the gathering dark. "He hurt Paw-Paw!" she cried. "I heard Paw-Paw cry."

Nikki remembered the yelp. "You might be right. We'd better go check."

Nikki found a torch in the shed, turned it on, took Mae by the hand, and led the way into the undergrowth.

"Paw-Paw, Paw-Paw!" Mae called softly.

"I'm not sure he'll come to us after what happened," said Nikki.

But at that very moment, Paw-Paw poked his head out from between two mountain laurel bushes and looked warily at the girls.

"It's OK, Paw-Paw. It's us," said Mae. "We won't hurt you." She held her hand towards his soft brown snout.

Nikki, moving slowly, extended her hand, too.

Paw-Paw sniffed the hands and finally emerged from the bushes.

"Are you all right?" said Mae.

Nikki passed the beam of the torch over Paw-Paw's body. "I see a scratch on his back, but that's all. He'll be OK."

"Shouldn't we put something on the scratch? Like a plaster?"

"Well, not a plaster. It would stick to his fur. But maybe some ointment or something. We'll have to wait, though. I'll try to do it later tonight. Maybe Tobias can help me when he gets home."

Mae nodded, then sat down, wrapped her arms

around Paw-Paw's neck and began to sob once again.

Nikki's father didn't stay awake long. He wanted to leave, he said, wanted to take the truck out again, but Tobias, who had returned by then, shoved his father on to the couch, where Mr Sherman immediately fell into a deep slumber.

"Good. He can sleep it off tonight. He won't wake up until the morning," said Tobias, who gave his father a look of disgust before heading out to his shed.

That was when Nikki did something she had never before done, not once in her life. She waited until her mother was putting Mae to bed, then tiptoed into the kitchen, checked to see if the phone was working and called a friend.

"I just needed to talk to you," said Nikki.

"I'm really glad you called," replied Olivia, who could count on the fingers of one hand the number of times she and Nikki had spoken on the telephone. "What's the matter?"

Nikki hesitated. She knew she couldn't relate the whole story to Olivia. Her mother had told her and Tobias and Mae many times that the authorities would come after them if they found out about Mr

Sherman. Nikki wasn't positive what that would mean, but it didn't sound like something she'd want to experience. So she focused on the dogs.

"There are just so many of them," she said to Olivia. "I can't keep up with their food. I don't have enough money."

"Won't your parents help you?" asked Olivia.

"They can't. They don't have enough money, either."

"Maybe I could help you. I've saved a little money from working at the store."

"Thanks," said Nikki, "but I really don't want money. I just wanted to talk to you. Cheer me up. Tell me something funny."

"Well. . ." said Olivia thoughtfully, "how about this: I got a little bit mad at my mom this afternoon – it's not important why – so I decided to play a trick on her. I took Sandy out of his cage, put him in the cookie jar, brought the jar into the living room and asked my mom if she wanted a cookie. When she lifted the lid, Sandy poked his head out and my mom screamed and fell off the couch."

Nikki giggled. "Didn't you get in trouble?"

"A little," admitted Olivia, "but it was worth it." She paused. "Did that make you feel better?"

"Yes," said Nikki.

"Then it was definitely worth it."

When Nikki and Olivia went to bed that night, each was smiling: Nikki because she had discovered the sweet pleasure of talking with a friend when she was having a bad time, and Olivia because she had been able to help her new friend.

17

The Fire at the Factory

When Flora had lived with her mother and father and Ruby in her old town, she had not known nearly as many people as she now knew in Camden Falls. There had been only a few families on her street, and they had not been as closely knit as the Row House neighbours. And when Flora had gone downtown, she barely knew anyone in the shops. She recognized the couple who ran the bookstore, and her mother was friendly with one of the women at the hair salon, but that was about it. It was a big town and people were busy and many of them, Flora reflected, didn't seem to have time for children. But in Camden Falls, partly because it was a small town and partly because of Min – where she lived and where she worked – Flora had a huge network of friends and an extended family.

And yet, there were times when Flora felt lonely. These were usually the afternoons when Ruby was at a rehearsal and Olivia was at a Whiz Kidz class and Nikki had gone home and couldn't come into town. Flora would walk into town after school by herself on those days, drift into Needle and Thread, and either begin her homework or pull out a sewing project. She knew she wasn't alone at these times, but still, she occasionally felt lonely.

On one of these afternoons, a drizzly day at the beginning of the second week in November, Flora flopped on to a couch in Needle and Thread and looked around the store. Her eyes fell on Mary's worktable, which Mary had tidied the last time she'd been in the store. Flora studied the rack that held Mary's spools of thread, arranged by colour, and the neatly laid out markers and scissors, measuring tape, pincushion and needle case. Sitting squarely in the middle of the table, Flora saw, was a paper bag with an index card taped to it. On the card was written *Mary*.

Flora stood up, threaded her way through the aisles of fabric to the worktable and peeked in the bag. She could see a pile of clothes, which she suspected needed to be hemmed or mended.

"Min?" said Flora.

Min was holding a bolt of fabric and discussing it with a young man who was frowning over a pattern. She glanced at Flora and held up one finger.

Flora waited patiently, then, when the man had gone off in search of thread, she said, "Min, I was just wondering – that package on Mary's table – would you like me to take it to her house?"

Min looked at Flora in surprise, but all she said was, "Thank you, Flora. I'm sure Mary would appreciate that. If you take it to her now, she'll be able to work on it at home, get a head start."

And so it was that ten minutes later, Flora Northrop was on her way to visit Mary Woolsey for the second time in her life. If anyone had asked her why, she wouldn't have known exactly what to say. She was simply aware that she frequently found herself thinking of her first visit with Mary – sitting in the little parlour with Daphne and Delilah, watching the cuckoo glide out of its painted house, listening to Mary talk about Flora's great-grandfather and the anonymous gifts of money. Flora knew there was much more to the story of Mary's life – and of Lyman Davis's and possibly her very own – and she wanted to hear it all.

Flora now made her way through Mary's gardens, which were even more stark and barren than when she had last visited. She paused at the top of the stone steps and gave the lion's head knocker three sharp raps.

The door opened a crack. "Who's there?" said Mary.

"It's me, Flora."

The door opened all the way, and there stood Mary Woolsey. "This is a surprise," she said.

Flora held out the bag. "Someone left this at the store and I thought you might like to have it today."

"Well, that was very thoughtful of you."

Mary took the bag, and for a moment Flora thought she was going to be sent on her way. She backed up a step.

"Would you like to come in?" asked Mary.

Flora shrugged. "OK. Sure."

They sat in the parlour again. Flora found Daphne and Delilah sleeping together in an armchair, and she squeezed in beside them. Mary settled herself on the couch.

"The last time I was here," said Flora, eyeing the cuckoo clock to see when she could expect it to chime, "you said my great-grandfather had been helping you out and that it was a very long story. Could you tell me that story?"

"Now?" replied Mary.

Flora nodded. "If you want to. It sounds like a good story, and I don't know much about my great-grandfather. I mean, I know what Min tells me, but a lot of things happened to her father before Min was born."

Mary leaned into the couch cushions and removed her glasses. "Well," she said, "in order to tell it, I have to go all the way back to nineteen twenty-nine. That's when the story really begins."

"Nineteen twenty-nine?" exclaimed Flora. "Really?"

Mary looked at her in surprise. "Yes. Why?"

Flora hesitated. "Remember the box I told you about? The one where I found the old photo of you and my mom?" (Mary nodded.) "There was a lot of other family stuff in there, too, including a whole bunch of letters that Min's mother had written. I don't know how they wound up back at our house, but anyway, they sort of tell this story about Min's father and something he did when there was that big stock market crash."

"How interesting," said Mary. "The stock market crash is part of my story, too. All right. Let me figure out how to start. I haven't told this story to anyone before." She folded her hands in her lap, stared out of the window, and then began to speak again.

"In nineteen twenty-nine, my mother, Leticia Woolsey, was just nineteen years old. She was employed as a maid at your house, Flora. She worked for your great-grandparents. Your grandmother and her sister hadn't been born yet, but their older brother had been. I believe he was about four in nineteen twenty-nine. My father, Ian, worked in an office in town, and he and my mother were expecting me. They didn't have a lot of money, but with two incomes, they weren't doing badly. My father was able to build this house and he even had a small savings.

"Then came the stock market crash. Your great-grandfather, as you may know, left his job shortly after that, and he also lost a lot of his own money. So he had to let my mother and two other maids and, of course, his office staff go. My mother had planned to stop working after I was born, so this wasn't much of a blow for her and my father. But something else was: your great-grandfather had convinced my father to invest his savings in the stock market. In fact, your great-grandfather had done the investing himself. So when the market crashed, not only did my mother lose her job earlier than she had planned, but my parents lost their entire savings. Then my father was let go from his job, too. Now my parents had no jobs, no savings, and a baby on the way."

"And it was all my great-grandfather's fault," said Flora in a whisper.

"Well, not entirely," replied Mary. "He couldn't have prevented the crash."

"I know. But still, I wonder. . ."

"What?" asked Mary. "What do you wonder?"

Flora shook her head. "Tell me what happened next."

"Well, a few months later, in nineteen thirty, I was born." Mary smiled at Flora. "Now you can figure out exactly how old I am."

Flora smiled back. "You're six years older than Min. That's not so old."

"Someone taught you excellent manners," said Mary, "and I suspect it was your parents." She turned a determined gaze on Flora. "I'm not one to tiptoe around things," she said. "Your parents must be mentioned."

Flora stroked Daphne's ears and nodded her head.

"Anyway, by nineteen thirty, when I was born, my parents had nothing except this house. They were practically destitute. Eventually, my father found work again, this time in a factory – it was the only job he could find – but our lives were still precarious. It was, after all, the Great Depression. And then one day," said Mary, "there was a fire at the factory. It was a horrible fire. The factory burned to the ground and many lives were lost. The families of the factory workers ran into town and waited there, hoping for news of their loved ones. My mother joined them. She waited and waited. At the end of the day, she went home and waited some more. My father didn't come back."

"That's awful!" cried Flora.

"The fire was a tragedy that affected Camden Falls for years," agreed Mary.

"What did your mother do?"

"She dug in and worked hard to support us. She was one of the hardest-working women I've ever known. She never married again, and she raised me to be independent. She said that in the end, the only person you can truly depend on is yourself. After the fire, my mother didn't reach out to others, and she taught me not to reach out to others, either. I'm afraid that what she created for us, finally, was a very insular life. Do you know what 'insular' means?"

"I think so," said Flora. "It means isolated, even

when you aren't really isolated." As she spoke these words, she found herself thinking of Nikki.

"That's a very interesting way of explaining it," replied Mary. "You do have a way with words, Flora. So – our life went on. I grew older. Our days became predictable. Then one day, several years after the fire – I suppose I must have been about seven, but I didn't know about this until many years later – something unexpected arrived in the mail."

"What was it?" asked Flora.

"An envelope. It was addressed to my mother, and inside she found an anonymous gift of money with a note that read simply, 'For Mary'."

"And it was from my great-grandfather?" asked Flora.

"Yes. But I didn't figure that out for a long time. In fact, my mother didn't even tell me about the money until I was eighteen. By then, there was quite a bit of it. The envelopes had kept arriving over the years, each containing cash and each with a note reading, 'For Mary'."

"Why did your mother wait so long to give you the money?"

"She wanted to be certain that I would handle it responsibly. It was quite a nest egg. My mother had deposited each gift in the bank, so the money had earned interest, too. The money was still arriving even after I turned eighteen, by the way. In fact, the gifts were still arriving – not as often, but every now and then – in the nineteen sixties. The last gift I received was in nineteen sixty-six. By then, the envelopes were addressed to me and not to my mother."

"You said you figured out for yourself that the money was from my great-grandfather. Didn't your mother tell you that?"

Mary shook her head. "All she would say was that the gifts were from an anonymous benefactor. And I didn't know enough about her past to have any idea who that might be."

"So how did you finally figure it out?" asked Flora, and she and both cats jumped when the cuckoo clock chimed. Flora turned to watch the bird, and she smiled when he retreated into his house.

"It was in nineteen seventy," said Mary. "I was forty and my mother had just died. I decided to clear some things out of the house and, just like you, I came across old letters and papers. When I discovered that my mother had worked for your family, I began to wonder about your great-grandfather. I did a little research on him. The more I learned – about his wealth and also about his reputation as a philanthropist – the more certain I became that he was the source of the money. I reasoned that he might feel guilty about what had happened to my family."

Flora said nothing.

"Flora?" asked Mary.

"Sorry. I was just thinking. This is so interesting. Do you realize that because of something my great-grandfather did almost eighty years ago, your life changed completely? If he hadn't fired your mother and lost your savings, well, for one thing, you might have grown up with your father, because he might not have been working at the factory."

When Mary didn't say anything, Flora continued. "Just think of all the people whose lives he must have changed – the other people he fired, the other people whose money he lost. What happened to them? I bet they have stories to tell, too. If I could find some of those people, maybe I could write about them for the three hundred and fiftieth birthday celebration. It would be a great project. Do you think you could help me with it?" asked Flora.

"What would you like me to do?"

"Well, you've already done a lot, telling me your story. But if you could think of anyone else I could talk to, that would be helpful."

"Descendants of the other people who knew your great-grandfather, that sort of thing?"

"Yes," said Flora. "If you want to. Only if you want to."

"Thank you," replied Mary. "I'll be happy to help you. Digging through the past can be very exciting. Just keep one thing in mind."

"OK," said Flora.

"Digging through the past can be painful, too," said Mary.

18

Sixteen for Dinner

"Min?" said Flora one evening. "Do you have a cable needle?" She held up a skein of off-white yarn and a pattern book. "I want to knit Nikki a pair of mittens for Christmas."

Min looked at the book. "Ah. Aran knits, with all the cables and designs. Flora, you are a much more accomplished knitter than I was at your age. My land. Yes, I think I have a cable needle somewhere." She fished through her knitting bag. "Here it is."

"Thank you," said Flora. "I might need just a little help with this pattern, but I think I can mostly make the mittens by myself."

It was a chilly evening, and Min had made a fire. She and Flora and Ruby and Daisy Dear and King Comma had gathered in front of it. Min's hands were busy smocking the sleeves of a baby dress.

("My friends keep on having grandchildren," she commented.) Ruby was lying on her back, one hand resting on Daisy Dear, whispering her lines from the school play.

Min looked over her reading glasses at Flora, who had begun to cast on the stitches for the first mitten. "Hard to believe it's already time to think about Christmas," she said. When neither girl answered her, she added, "You know, Thanksgiving is just two weeks away now... Girls?"

"I don't want to talk about it," said Ruby.

"I'm afraid we must talk about it," replied Min. "We can't ignore it. You're going to have two days off from school, and the store will be closed on Thursday. We can't just sit here and pretend it isn't Thanksgiving."

"I could," said Ruby, rolling over and staring into the fire.

"No, that's silly," said Flora. "Min's right. We can't ignore Thanksgiving."

"But what are we going to *do*?" asked Ruby. "Min, you said yourself that you've forgotten how to cook a turkey."

"Well, that was a bit of an exaggeration."

"But it would be so sad, just the three of us, here instead of at home – I mean, instead of at our old home, without Mom and Dad. . ." Flora set her knitting down and pulled King Comma into her lap.

"I agree," said Min. "And that's why I was thinking that maybe we could do something different, something that wouldn't remind us so much of what we were missing. We could have dinner in a restaurant. The Fig Tree has a very fancy Thanksgiving dinner menu. Or maybe we could go away for a few days, after Ruby's performance. I could line up some extra help at the store."

"Where would we go?" asked Flora.

"Could we go to Disney World?" asked Ruby with sudden interest.

"I think it's a bit late to plan that," said Min, "but maybe we could find a nice bed-and-breakfast in Vermont or New Hampshire."

"OK, but no educational vacations," said Ruby. "I don't want to be dragging through museums, learning about Pilgrims and maize."

"I promise it would be a fun trip, and we would have Thanksgiving dinner at an inn, and it would be cosy and lovely, but it wouldn't remind us of other years. How does that sound?" asked Min.

"Fine," said Flora.

"Fine," said Ruby.

"OK. I'll make some telephone calls tomorrow and see what I can come up with."

"Could you call Disney World while you're at it?" asked Ruby.

The next evening, soon after dinner had ended, the doorbell rang.

Daisy erupted into loud and frantic barking, which caused King Comma to fly out of the kitchen and skid around a corner, sending a throw rug under a table.

"My stars and garters," said Min as she dried her hands on a dish towel. She followed Daisy to the door and held on to the dog's collar as she peeked through the window. "Bill!" she exclaimed. She opened the door and let Mr Willet in. "How nice to see you."

"Sorry to drop by unannounced," he said, "but Barbara Fong came over to stay with Mary Lou for a bit, so I thought I'd take advantage of her visit to get out of the house. I hope I'm not interrupting dinner."

"No, we've just finished," said Min. "Make yourself at home."

Mr Willet sat down in the living room, and Daisy, who now recognized him as a friend, jumped on to the couch, turned around twice, and lay beside him, pressing her back against his legs.

"Isn't this nice?" said Mr Willet. "Hello, girls," he added as Flora and Ruby joined them.

Min made tea, Flora and Ruby lay reading by the fire, and the grown-ups began to talk. Flora paid little attention until she heard the words "nursing home". Then she laid her book down and sat up to listen.

"I just can't care for her at home any more," Mr Willet was telling Min. "Mary Lou needs too much help. She needs help dressing and bathing, and I'm not strong enough to lift her any more."

"What about hiring a nurse?" suggested Min.

"I've thought about that, but I don't know. We'd need round-the-clock help. I think Mary Lou will be safer in a nursing home. Right now, she's up half the night wandering around. I'm afraid she's going to leave the house or turn on the stove. It's getting dangerous."

Min rested her hand on Mr Willet's arm. "I'm so sorry," she said. "You've been wonderful neighbours and dear friends. We'll miss Mary Lou very much. I can't imagine how sad this must be for you."

Mr Willet nodded, his eyes bright. "Luckily, there are several nursing homes not far away, plus a fine continuing-care retirement community with a wing for people with Alzheimer's. That's where I'd like Mary Lou to go, but there won't be space available until after the holidays. We'll just have to muddle through until then."

"Bill," said Min, "what are you and Mary Lou going to do for Thanksgiving?"

"Oh." Mr Willet put his hand to his forehead. "I'd almost forgotten about Thanksgiving. We don't have any plans. I've been so preoccupied."

"Well," said Min, and she looked at Flora and Ruby, "we don't have any plans, either. We were thinking of going away for a few days, but—"

"But could you have Thanksgiving with us?" asked Ruby.

"Please?" said Flora.

"Why, we'd love to," replied Mr Willet. "That would be wonderful. What a lovely offer. Thank you so much."

"Well, now," said Min later as she closed the door behind Mr Willet, "isn't that nice? We'll stay home after all. Five for Thanksgiving. That seems more festive."

Late the next afternoon, as Ruby and Flora and Min were walking home from Needle and Thread, Min said, "You'll never guess what. I was talking to Olivia's mother today and she mentioned that the Walters were going to spend Thanksgiving in New York City, but now they've decided to stay here in order to save money. So I invited them to join us for dinner."

"Really?" cried Flora. "Olivia's family is coming, too?"

"Then that's ten people!" said Ruby. "Excellent."

"We never had ten people for Thanksgiving," said Flora. "This is going to be fun. How are we going to fit everyone in the dining room, though?"

"Oh, don't worry. We'll think of something. That's part of the fun," replied Min.

"Min? What does Mr Pennington do on Thanksgiving?" asked Ruby.

"Goodness me, I don't know. I'd better ask him."

"Hey! I just had a brilliant idea!" exclaimed Flora. "We could have a Row House Thanksgiving. You said you have Row House parties sometimes, and we had the barbecue last summer, remember? That was great. What if we invited everyone else in the Row Houses?"

"Well. . ." Min paused. "Now, that *would* be a lot of people."

"Everyone could bring something," Flora went on, "so you wouldn't have to do all the cooking, Min."

"It would be very festive and Thanksgiving-y," said Ruby.

"We'd help you," said Flora. "We'd do whatever you asked."

So that night, Min phoned Mr Pennington, the Morrises, the Edwardses, the Malones, and the Fongs. The Morrises and the Malones planned to be away for the holiday, but everyone else was excited about Thanksgiving at Min's house.

"Now it's *sixteen* people!" said Ruby.

"Lordy me," said Min.

"Um, Min? Could we ask Nikki's family, too?" Flora looked pleadingly at her grandmother.

"You're going to phone Nikki's house?" said Ruby incredulously.

"Only if Min says it's OK."

"It's fine," said Min. "That's a very nice idea, Flora."

"But, Flora, what if Nikki's father answers the phone?" said Ruby.

"Do you want *me* to invite the Shermans?" asked Min.

"No. I'll do it," replied Flora, but she could already

feel her heart starting to pound. "I'll do it right now before I lose my nerve."

Flora took the phone into her bedroom and shut the door. Fingers trembling, she punched in Nikki's number. She held her breath.

"Hello?" said a small voice.

"Mae?" said Flora, and she relaxed.

"Yes. Who's speaking, please?"

"It's Flora, Nikki's friend. Is Nikki there?"

"Yes." Flora heard a loud thump, as if Mae had dropped the phone. Then she heard muffled voices, and finally Nikki, sounding surprised, said, "Flora?"

"Yup. It's me. Nikki, I wanted to ask you something. Min and Ruby and I decided to have all these people over for Thanksgiving. At first we weren't going to do anything at all, but then we decided to invite our friends for dinner. Olivia and her family will be here, and we wanted to know if you and your family could come, too. Do you have any plans?"

Nikki let a sigh escape. At last she said, "I'm pretty sure we don't have any plans. I have no idea what we're going to do. But this isn't, um, this isn't . . . I'm sort of in trouble with my father. I'd better not ask him about anything right now."

"Can't you ask your mother?"

"Yes, but then she'd just have to ask my father, and I'm sorry, Flora – I know this is hard to understand – it's hard to explain, too. But if either Mom or I ask my father if we can go to your house for Thanksgiving, he's going to say no because he's mad at me."

"But the invitation is for your whole family, not just you."

"I know. I said this was hard to explain."

"Why is your father mad at you?" asked Flora finally.

"Because I disobeyed him. Look, Flora, I can't really talk right now." Nikki lowered her voice to a whisper. "I have to go," she said quickly, and hung up the phone.

Flora was disappointed until she thought of the sixteen people who would gather at her house for Thanksgiving, and then her spirits rose again. In the store the next day, she invited Mary Woolsey to dinner, too, but Mary said shyly that no, no, she couldn't accept, but thank you very much, Flora, thank you.

Still and all. Sixteen for Thanksgiving dinner. Flora and Ruby and Min got busy with their plans.

19

Goodbye and Hello

Thanksgiving, thought Olivia, used to be . . . what was the word? Simple? No, that wasn't quite right. But it was sort of right. Up until this year, whenever Thanksgiving rolled around, Olivia and her family made plans for the holiday, gave thanks and ate their meal. There was usually plenty to give thanks for, and Olivia looked forward to the holiday, celebrated it, then went back to school and continued with her autumn.

But this year was different. This year, the Walters had planned to go to New York City for Thanksgiving. They had started talking about the trip nearly a year earlier. They were going to stay in a hotel, watch the Macy's parade from the windows of their hotel rooms, eat dinner in a restaurant and go to a show on Broadway. Olivia had been looking forward to this for months and months. Then her father lost his job. At first, the Walters thought they could go ahead with the trip. Surely one of Olivia's parents would find work soon. But this hadn't happened, and finally a family meeting had been called at which it was announced that the trip was off. Disappointment.

Then Min had invited the Walters to what had turned into a big Row House Thanksgiving celebration. Olivia was excited again.

Her excitement faded, however, when she thought about Mrs Mandel. On the last day of school before Thanksgiving vacation, Olivia and her classmates were going to hold their party to say goodbye to their favourite teacher ever. The party would be fun, and Mr Donaldson, who had visited Olivia's class several times now, seemed nice, so Olivia was looking forward to welcoming him. But how could she say goodbye to Mrs Mandel?

Thanksgiving this year reminded Olivia of a picture book she had liked when she was little. It was called *Fortunately, Unfortunately*. And that was her Thanksgiving, all right. Fortunately, she and her family had had a big trip planned. Unfortunately, they had to cancel the trip. Fortunately, Min invited them to dinner. Unfortunately, Olivia's favourite teacher was retiring the day before. Fortunately, her goodbye party would be fun. And on and on. Olivia hoped this wasn't part of growing up. She didn't like complications.

On the day of the party, Olivia, Ruby and Flora met Nikki's bus as usual. The girls walked Mae to her classroom and Ruby to hers, then slowly approached Mrs Mandel's room.

"I guess this is it," said Flora.

"I can't believe we have to say goodbye to Mrs Mandel," said Olivia. "I waited six years for her to be my teacher."

"Remember how happy we were on the day we found out we were going to be in her class together?" said Nikki.

Olivia peeped into the classroom. Then she ducked back. "Mrs Mandel and Mr Donaldson are both in there already," she said in a loud whisper.

The girls flattened themselves against the wall.

"Do you think the party is going to be a complete surprise?" asked Flora.

"I hope so," said Nikki.

"It better be," said Olivia. Olivia's classmates and their parents had worked hard planning the party – and keeping it a secret. "Now I know what you must have gone through to plan my big one-oh," said

Olivia. She thought about what was supposed to happen that afternoon, and she shivered.

"Well ... I guess we should go inside," said Nikki.

"Wait!" cried Olivia softly. "Where are your gifts? Did you guys remember your gifts?"

"Min's bringing mine this afternoon," said Flora. "I was afraid Mrs Mandel and Mr Donaldson would see them before the party if I brought them."

Nikki patted her new backpack, a recent gift from Mrs DuVane. "Mine are in here. My parents aren't coming today."

"Oh, not even your mother?" asked Olivia.

"Nope."

"But why isn't your mother coming?"

"My father won't let her. Not for this. He's still punishing me."

Olivia felt like saying "I hate him" but kept her mouth closed. Instead, she put her arm around her friend and said, "You can borrow my mom and dad."

"And Min and Mr Pennington," said Flora. Then she added, "Mr Pennington is really excited about the party. Did you know he used to teach here years and years and years ago, before he was principal at the high school?"

"Really?" said Nikki. "Well, thanks, you guys. Maybe if we all just hang around together, no one will even notice that my parents didn't come."

Olivia put her hand on the doorknob. "OK," she said, "let's go."

The girls entered their room. Mrs Mandel and Mr Donaldson were standing together in front of the blackboard.

"Good morning," said Mrs Mandel, and Olivia suddenly had the horrible feeling that she was going to burst into tears right there in front of her class. She pressed her lips together, though, and the feeling passed.

The day passed, too, and it didn't drag the way days with parties or surprises at the end usually do. Olivia was slightly disappointed. She had hoped for one long, last delicious day with Mrs Mandel. But before she knew it, the bell had rung for lunch time, and soon enough, both lunch and recess were over and she and her classmates were back in their seats.

The surprise was about to begin. Olivia found herself holding her breath. She and Nikki and Flora kept exchanging looks, then glancing at the door to their classroom. If all went as planned, Mr Giordano, who worked in the school office, should appear at any moment.

And suddenly, there he was. He rapped twice on the door, then let himself inside. "Excuse me," he said quietly, taking Mrs Mandel and Mr Donaldson aside. (Olivia clapped her hand over her mouth. She didn't want to do anything to ruin the surprise now.) "Could you go to the office for a few moments? Mrs Covey needs to see you."

"Both of us?" asked Mrs Mandel.

"Just for a minute. I'll stay here with your class."

Looking puzzled, Mrs Mandel and Mr Donaldson left the room. Mr Giordano winked at the kids, then put a finger to his lips. Finally, he peered into the hallway. When he reappeared, he said, "OK, Olivia, you can go to the front door and tell everyone to come in."

"Me?!" squeaked Olivia. She hadn't known this big job would be given to her. Remembering not to run, she strode down the hall and flung open the door. Standing in the car park were the parents and grandparents and other party guests. "Come in!" cried Olivia.

Several minutes later, Mrs Mandel and Mr Donaldson returned to the classroom. They opened the door.

"SURPRISE!" shouted a roomful of people.

Mrs Mandel put her hand on her chest and opened her mouth but didn't say a word. Mr Donaldson just stared.

"I think they're really surprised, don't you?" Olivia asked Nikki.

"Definitely."

Mrs Mandel plopped down into her desk chair for a moment. While she recovered, Olivia's mother made a speech. "You were my favourite teacher," she said, "and now you're my daughter's favourite teacher. We have all been lucky to have you in our school and our lives and our hearts." (At this, Mrs Mandel had to start a search for some Kleenex.) "We understand, though, that things change. Your family needs you now. So we say goodbye, knowing that we're better people because of you. And we say welcome to *you*." (Mrs Walter nodded towards Mr Donaldson.) "We're glad you've joined the Camden Falls Elementary community."

After this, Olivia remembered lots of laughing and crying and applauding and hugging, all in a rush like a giant ocean wave. Then Flora, who had been elected for the job, stood at the front of the room and nervously read the sentence she'd prepared: "Mrs Mandel, because we're going to miss you, and

Mr Donaldson, because we welcome you, we've made you some presents."

Olivia and her classmates produced their gifts, each accompanied by a card or letter. Packages were pulled out of desks and backpacks and coat pockets and out of shopping bags that had arrived with parents.

Mrs Mandel looked at the growing mound of presents on the desk. "You made all of these things?" she said. "I'm overcome."

Mrs Mandel and Mr Donaldson spent the rest of the party opening the gifts while refreshments were served. Every so often, Mrs Mandel would hold up a painting or a clay dish and say, "I absolutely can't believe this is handmade." And Mr Donaldson, sifting through his stack of paintings and drawings, said at last, "We'll have to create an art gallery in our room for all your beautiful work."

Olivia smiled at her parents, Nikki held Mr Pennington's hand, Flora showed Min around the room. It was a lovely party, Olivia thought, and not as sad as she had feared it would be. At the end of the day, shortly before the last bell rang, Mrs Mandel said, "Boys and girls, now I have something for you." She opened her desk drawer and pulled out a stack of envelopes. "I wrote each of you a personal letter. You may read the letters when you're at home." She began to hand out the envelopes. "You've been a wonderful, inspiring class, and I'm going to miss you." Later, when the party was over, Mrs Mandel hugged her students as they filed out of the door.

Olivia burst into tears when Mrs Mandel hugged her, and her teacher smiled and said, "Remember to read your letter."

Olivia waited until after dinner that evening. She took the letter to her bedroom, shut the door behind her and opened the envelope. Inside, on pale blue paper decorated with hummingbirds, were written the following words:

Dear Olivia,
These are the things I like about you:
1. Your gift for science
2. Your energy
3. Your spirit
4. Your strength
5. Your enthusiasm
You are a remarkable person and I will miss you.
Your teacher,
　　Mrs Mandel

Olivia tucked the letter in her treasure box. When she found it there several years later, she moved it to her desk drawer. She took it to college with her, and as an adult, she always knew where the letter was.

20

The First Thanksgiving

When Ruby thought about it, she realized there aren't a lot of Thanksgiving songs. There are a few hymns of thanksgiving, but as a holiday, Thanksgiving isn't as musically rich as Christmas. Ruby could even think of some Halloween songs, but Thanksgiving – well, it certainly wasn't anything like Christmas when it came to music. Which was why Ruby had been surprised to learn that the first time the Camden Falls Children's Chorus would give a performance would be at the Thanksgiving service at the community centre, and that they would not be singing hymns.

Ruby tried to be polite when she heard this news. She raised her hand (instead of calling out).

"Yes?" said Ms Angelo, the director of the chorus.

Ruby, standing third from the right in the second

row, lowered her hand. "What will we be singing?" she asked.

"We're going to perform two of the songs we've been rehearsing this fall: 'You're Never Fully Dressed Without a Smile' and 'Winter Wonderland'. Two upbeat songs, one of them about winter – because believe it or not, winter is almost here."

Ruby was elated. "You're Never Fully Dressed Without a Smile" was from *Annie*. Maybe Ruby would even be given a solo part.

As it turned out, Ruby did not have a solo. For the first performance of the new season, no one did. "There will be plenty of solos in future performances," said Ms Angelo. "But this is our first, and we just need to practise singing and working together and being in front of an audience."

Still, Ruby was excited about their concert. Thanksgiving, in fact, was going to be a big day – first the service at the community centre, then the dinner that Min had organized. So Ruby was disappointed to discover, when she joined Min and Flora in the kitchen on Thanksgiving morning, that Flora was near tears.

"What's the matter?" Ruby asked her sister.

"What do you *think* is the matter?" was the sniffly reply.

"Flora," said Min, "I know you're sad, but do you think you could use kind words when you address Ruby? All she did was ask you a question. I'm very sorry you're upset, but if you're going to be rude as well, you need to go back to your room."

"Sorry," said Flora. "I mean, I really am sorry."

"We do have a lot to look forward to today, you know," said Min. "We also have a lot to do. If you want to take your mind off things, you can help me with the scalloped potatoes. I've never made scalloped potatoes for sixteen people before. Thank goodness I'm not in charge of the turkey. Now, where did I put those jars of olives?" Min began searching through cupboards. "My land, I just remembered, I'll need to put out butter, too – on both tables. Oh! Girls, did you make the place cards yet?"

Ruby started to giggle, and Flora smiled. Then Ruby sniffed the air. "What do I smell?" she asked.

Min made a dash for the oven. "Sticky buns!" she exclaimed, rescuing them from the oven. "Now, why did I think I would have time to make sticky buns this morning?"

"Yum," said Ruby. "I'm glad you did."

Ruby and Flora and Min sat down to a quick breakfast of Min's home-made buns. When they were finished, Min said, "Now, we need to make sure the tables are ready for this afternoon. The service starts at eleven, and everyone will arrive for dinner at two, so we won't have time to do much in between. Come look at the tables with me."

The dining room table, with the leaf added, was to be set for ten people. In the living room, two card tables had been joined together, covered with a tablecloth, and would be set for six people.

"What do you think?" asked Min.

"They're going to look beautiful," replied Ruby.

"There's just one problem," said Flora. "The dining room table is for the adults, right? And if you leave things this way, Robby winds up eating at the kids' table."

"Oh, dear," said Min. "You're right, Flora."

"I have an idea," said Ruby. "When Robby and his parents arrive, you could say, 'Hi, Robby. Happy Thanksgiving! I have a question for you. Could I put you in charge of the kids' table in the living room?' You could seat him at the head of the table. I bet he'll want to eat with us."

"*We* want him to eat with us," said Flora.

"Good thinking, Ruby," said Min. "Here, why don't you and Flora put out the place cards in the living room, and I'll put them out in the dining room?"

"Flora, can you do it?" asked Ruby. "I have to get ready for the performance. We have to be at the community centre early. Mrs Longyear is going to pick me up. She's going to drive Ava and me since the Morrises are away."

Ruby ran upstairs and dressed in the white blouse and navy skirt that Min had pressed for her the night before. Everyone in the chorus would be wearing a white shirt or blouse and navy trousers or a skirt. Ruby pictured Min and Flora seated in the community centre, looking at the sea of navy and white on the risers at the front of the room.

Ruby lay on the floor. She did a few yoga exercises. Then she stood up and sang both of the songs they would be performing. The songs were to be sung from memory. No sheet music allowed. (No musical accompaniment, either.) Ruby checked herself in the mirror once more. She was ready.

The community centre, a large shingled structure just outside of town, had been decorated for Thanksgiving. Ruby drew in her breath when she stepped through the double doors. The last time she had been there, for a rehearsal, the centre had seemed cavernous and dim. Now, in the light of a November morning, it seemed friendlier. And to Ruby's delight, sheaves of dried corn adorned the end of each row of seats. In the front of the room were enormous arrangements of autumn flowers, and on a table was a cornucopia, gourds and vegetables spilling from it across a pumpkin-coloured tablecloth.

The members of the Children's Chorus waited in a room near the back door of the centre while the Thanksgiving service began. Ruby could hear music playing, and someone with a very deep voice talking about blessings, and then more music. Min and Flora, she knew, were sitting with Mr Pennington somewhere near the front of the main hall, Mr Pennington in his three-piece suit, Min in her very best trouser suit, and Flora wearing a dress she had made mostly by herself.

"Kids? Ready? It's time to go," said Ms Angelo at last, and Ruby was surprised to find that she felt nervous.

With Ms Angelo leading the way, the members of the Camden Falls Children's Chorus filed into the main hall and on to the risers at the front, just as they had rehearsed. When they were standing in their places in four neat lines, Ms Angelo waited until all the rustling and shifting around had stopped. She smiled at her students. Then she played a single note on the piano and raised her arms. In clear voices,

Ruby and the chorus began "Winter Wonderland". The audience was hushed, the only sound in the centre the confident notes of the members of the chorus. Ruby looked out into the audience, lit by sunshine filtering through the tall windows, and tried to find Min and Flora and Mr Pennington. There they were. Ruby flashed them a smile, and Min and Mr Pennington smiled back at her. Flora gave her a quick thumbs-up sign.

Ruby shivered. Outside, the day was blustery. Inside, the centre was warm, and she was surrounded by friends and family and music and tradition and peace. She smiled especially widely as she sang, ". . . *but brother, you're never fully dressed without a smile!*"

Two hours later, the service over, Ruby was at home waiting with Flora and Min for their Thanksgiving guests to arrive. She had changed out of her skirt and blouse and was wearing a jumper that Min had made for her.

"You girls are a picture," said Min, standing back to survey her granddaughters.

"Thank you," said Ruby.

Flora studied the tables, which were now ready for the feast. They were laid with Min's best china, her silver, and her crystal. A place card stood at each dinner plate. Fresh flowers had been arranged in vases. Dishes of olives and nuts had been set out.

"Min," said Flora, "everything looks wonderful, but I've never seen so many forks and spoons and knives. There are two of each at every place. How will we know which ones to use when?"

"Don't worry about that," said Min. "It's partly for show. Do you know whose china and silver this is?"

Ruby and Flora shook their heads.

"It was my great-grandmother's originally, and it's been passed down to each generation. Someday it will be yours."

"Your great-grandmother's!" exclaimed Flora. "That would be my great-great-great-grandmother's."

The doorbell rang then, and Ruby cried, "The first guests! Let me answer it!"

She opened the door to Mr and Mrs Fong, each holding a covered dish.

"Happy Thanksgiving!" said Ruby.

"Happy Thanksgiving," they replied.

In no time, the rest of the guests had arrived, and Min's house was filled with talking and laughter and good smells and neighbours in their best clothes. Robby, wearing a suit and tie, had already agreed to be in charge of the kids and had draped his jacket over the chair at the head of the table in the living room.

Min had made spiced cider, and Mr Fong was in charge of serving it. Mr and Mrs Edwards helped Min in the kitchen. Olivia's mother passed around hors d'oeuvres she had made. The Willets sat on the couch by the fire, Mr Pennington across from them. Jack and Henry ran around and around the house until their father gave them a pad of paper and a pencil and asked them to find out what everyone wanted to drink with dinner. Ruby, Flora and Olivia sat by themselves with plates of hors d'oeuvres, ankles crossed delicately, and pretended they were at a ball at the governor's mansion. And Daisy Dear lay down under the dining room table, knowing that food would soon be served, while King Comma hid on the bottom shelf of a bookcase, eyes round and hackles raised.

When dinner was finally ready and everyone was seated, Min stood at the head of the table in the dining room and said, "Ruby and Flora and I want to thank you for joining us on our first Thanksgiving together in Camden Falls. We're happy that you're able to celebrate it with us, and we're grateful to be surrounded by such wonderful friends. And such wonderful food," she added, surveying the table, which was laden with steaming dishes.

Ruby, looking at her sister, at Robby, at Olivia and her brothers, and then at the adults seated in the dining room – at all the smiling faces turned to Min – forgot for a moment that this was a different Thanksgiving from any she had known and thought only that this was a happy moment that she would hold in her heart.

21

Night-time

If you were to walk down Main Street at the end of Thanksgiving Day in the year that Flora and Ruby Northrop moved to Camden Falls, you would find it nearly deserted. Lights are on in most of the shop-windows, though, so the street looks cheerful. The only person in sight is Sonny Sutphin in his wheelchair, making his way home. He didn't have anyone to share Thanksgiving with, and he wanted to get out for a breath of air and the familiar sights of Main Street before he retired for the evening. It's been a long, lonely day. Sonny pauses to look in each window as he passes, grateful that the next day is not a holiday and town will be busy again.

Now, if you were to walk out of town and along the country roads to Nikki Sherman's house, you would find, on this Thanksgiving evening, a happier family than usual. Mr Sherman has been on his best behaviour all day and has had nothing, not even a beer, to drink. Furthermore, the night before, when Tobias opened the front door and found on the stoop a large basket containing a smoked turkey and cans of vegetables and a bag of rolls and everything one might need for a Thanksgiving dinner, Mr Sherman allowed it to be brought inside and appreciated. There was no note with the basket, which Nikki suspects is from Mrs DuVane, and this is the kind of charitable act which is apt to anger her father. But he said nothing about the old bat or the basket – not the night before, and not today – and the Shermans have enjoyed an actual Thanksgiving dinner at their kitchen table, and even better, a day with no fighting. Nikki doesn't expect this to last, but she is thankful, extremely thankful, for one day of peace and quiet, not to mention her very full belly.

Now walk back to town. The country roads are quiet. There is almost no traffic this evening, but a stiff wind is blowing, and every now and then a coyote can be heard howling in the distant hills. Walk along Main Street again. Sonny Sutphin is gone, and the only living thing in sight is a skinny scared kitten who has discovered that Sharon leaves dishes of food and water outside the door to the Cheshire Cat.

Turn left at Dutch Haus, then right on Aiken Avenue, and there are the Row Houses. Tonight two of them are dark. The Morrises and the Malones will not be returning from their Thanksgiving holidays until Sunday. But lights are on in the other six homes.

If you peek into the Fongs' house, you'll find Barbara and Marcus standing in the middle of the room on the first floor that they have decided will be their baby's nursery.

"It's not too early to start thinking about decorating it, is it?" asks Barbara.

Marcus grins. "I don't think so."

"We could paint murals on the walls."

"I like that idea. What about jungle animals?"

"Or sea creatures?"

"What should our colour scheme be?"

"Yellow and green," says Barbara. "And blue."

"Pastel colours."

"I was thinking that I could make pillows and bumper covers and all sorts of wonderful fabric things for the room."

Next door, Robby and his parents are seated at their kitchen table. Mr and Mrs Edwards are drinking coffee from their HIS and HERS mugs, and Robby is making turkey sandwiches for their supper with some of the leftovers Min gave her guests as they were leaving.

"I'm always so stuffed after Thanksgiving dinner that I think I'll never be able to eat again," says Mr Edwards. "And then by supper time I'm ready for a turkey sandwich."

"I'm making my secret sauce," says Robby, his back to his parents. "Don't look over here while I'm cooking." He's busy with mayonnaise and mustard.

When the sandwiches are ready, he serves them to his parents, and his mother says, "Robby, your dad and I have been talking. We've spoken with Mrs Fulton, too, and we've decided that if you want to get a job after graduation, that will be fine."

"Really?!" exclaims Robby.

"Really. Mrs Fulton will help us look into things."

"Sweet!" says Robby.

On the other side of Robby's house, Mr Pennington is standing in his kitchen, looking over the container of leftovers from Min's. He selects a piece of turkey, places it on a plate and cuts off several pieces, which he puts in Jacques's dish. Then he adds broccoli and scalloped potatoes to his own plate.

"Here, boy!" calls Mr Pennington.

He sits down in the kitchen with his snack, Jacques at his feet with his own snack, and is just about to take a bite when the phone rings.

"Hello?" says Mr Pennington.

"Happy Thanksgiving, Dad!" says the voice at the end of the phone.

At the Walters' house, everyone has gathered in the living room, where Mrs Walter has made a fire. Henry and Jack are playing with their Game Boys, thrilled that they have three entire free days left before school starts again. Olivia is on the couch, wedged in between her parents, with Sandy in her lap. She's thinking not of the "unfortunatelys", not of the secret she's keeping for Mr Pennington, not of saying goodbye to Mrs Mandel, but of the holidays and what the next few weeks will bring.

"I can't believe you're going to go to work tomorrow, Mom," she says. "When was the last time you went to work?"

"Just before you were born. I was a gift wrapper at LaVake's over in Kingston."

"Did you like it?"

"I loved it. It was very creative. And I learned a lot about retail when I was there."

Mrs Walter has got a temporary job helping Mrs

Grindle at Stuff 'n' Nonsense during the busy Christmas season.

"Now when Flora and Ruby go to Needle and Thread after school, I can come visit you," says Olivia. "It'll be fun, even if Mrs Grindle is a little . . ." (she glances at her mother) "a little stern."

"Maybe I can lighten the mood in there," says Mrs Walter.

Three doors away, Mr and Mrs Willet are having a pleasantly quiet evening. For the first time in many months, Mrs Willet has neither argued nor protested when her husband said it was time to get ready for bed. Mr Willet doesn't know why this is so, but he isn't going to spend time wondering about it. Mrs Willet allowed him to help her into her nightgown and to brush her teeth, and now they're sitting in front of the television, watching the original *Miracle on 34th Street*.

"My, that Natalie Wood is a wonderful little actress," says Mrs Willet. "She'll go on to do big things."

Mr Willet is surprised that his wife has recognized Natalie Wood and even more surprised that she has remembered her name. But he feels only a crushing sadness because he realizes that Mrs Willet thinks this old movie is current.

"Dear, how old are you?" Mr Willet asks his wife suddenly.

She looks confused for a moment, then guesses, "Thirty-four?"

The Willets' Row House is the second from the left. Now walk back to the house that's the fourth from the left, sandwiched between the Malones' and the Walters'. Here are Flora and Ruby and Min, still cleaning up long after their guests have gone. Ruby's thoughts are on Christmas, but Flora's are on her family. As she puts away yet another plate that she now knows once belonged to her great-great-great-grandmother, she says, "Min? Have you really lived in this Row House your entire life?"

"Well, not my entire life. When I got married, my parents were still living here, and your grandfather and I wanted a place of our own. So we rented an apartment in Stanfield. But when Mother and Father moved to Florida, we moved back here. And I've been here ever since."

"How long did your parents live in Florida?"

"Let me see," says Min. She sets aside her sponge and sits at the kitchen table to think. "My father only lived there for about three years. He died unexpectedly in nineteen sixty-four. But my mother lived there for more than twenty years."

Flora and Ruby and Min return to their cleaning and tidying, Flora's mind on her family and her ancestors. It isn't until she is lying in bed later that night, about to drift off to sleep, that something occurs to her. Min said her father died in nineteen sixty-four. Flora is almost positive that's what she said. She's also almost positive that Mary Woolsey said, during Flora's last visit, that she received her final gift of money from her anonymous benefactor in nineteen sixty-six. If that's so, then it couldn't have come from Flora's great-grandfather. Maybe, thinks Flora, it came from her great-grandmother. But that doesn't seem right. Mary barely mentioned Min's mother.

So . . . if Mary's benefactor wasn't Flora's great-grandfather, who was?

Flora turns this question over and over in her mind until she finally slides into sleep, and another Camden Falls evening comes to an end.

Continue your walk down

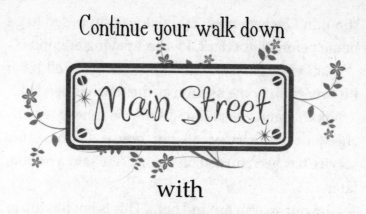

with

'Tis the Season

Outside Flora could see that the street was even more crowded than before. People were streaming by Needle and Thread, all hurrying in the same direction.

Olivia was grinning. "This is almost as good as what happens on Christmas Eve. You didn't know about this, did you?" she said to Flora and Ruby.

They shook their heads.

And Nikki added, "I've heard about it, but I've never seen it."

'You're kidding," said Olivia. "I thought you lived here all your life."

"I have. But we never came into town for this. In fact," Nikki went on, looking worried, "I probably shouldn't be here now. I think I was supposed to go home before it got dark. I wasn't paying attention."

"Call your parents," said Gigi gently. "Tell them I'll drive you home as soon as the tree has been lit."

Nikki, hands shaking, used the phone at the checkout counter to call her house. "I think the service has been turned off again," she said a minute later.

Gigi put an arm around her. "This is not for you to worry about. Come with us and enjoy the ceremony. Min and I will take care of things."

"OK. Thank you," said Nikki.

Min was walking around the store, turning off sewing machines and unplugging irons and the coffee pot. "Will you join us, Mary?" she said as Mary slipped into her coat.

Mary bowed her head. "I think I'll head on home."

Even Flora knew better than to beg her to stay. But she did say, "I'll see you next week. Keep thinking about our mystery!"

At last, the store lights were turned off, too, except for the tiny gold ones that now bordered the window, and Min, Gigi, Flora, Ruby, Olivia and Nikki stepped into the frosty night air. They joined the crowd moving along the pavement, sleeves brushing sleeves, mittened hands raised in greetings, boots tromping. Every business had closed, Flora realized, but the streetlights glowed, and the windows were alive with mechanical Santas and trimmed trees and glowing stars. Flora passed several menorahs, the candles still unlit as the first night of Hanukkah was two weeks away. As she paused by some windows, she heard music – songs and carols and bells chiming – and as she paused by others, she smelled chocolate and cider and warm buttery things.

"Ooh, look!" Ruby said suddenly.

They had reached the town square. A fir tree, at least three storeys high, had been placed in the centre of the square. Its branches were dark, but Flora could see the lights that had been twined around them, and she could smell the sharp scent that made her feel as if she were deep in a pine forest. In front of the tree a group of carollers, each holding a candle, stood in a tight knot, voices raised. "*Adeste fideles!*" they sang.

"'Everywhere, everywhere, Christmas tonight'," murmured Flora, remembering a poem she had once read.

And at that, Nikki cried out, "Mom!" She broke away from Flora and Ruby and Olivia and wiggled through the crowd of people.

"Hey, there's Mae," said Olivia, pointing to Nikki's little sister.

"And Tobias," added Flora.

"And I guess that's Mrs Sherman," said Ruby.

The carollers stopped singing then, and one of them stepped forward and led the crowd in "Deck the Halls" and "Silent Night". There was a moment of expectant silence, and then a tree of blue and green and gold and red and violet and white sprang forth from the darkness.

Flora drew in her breath. It's like magic, she thought. But years later, even when she was a grown woman remembering this Christmas in Camden Falls, the image that would first come into her mind was not of the tree but of Nikki standing between her mother and Mae, holding their hands, Tobias behind them, their faces shining, Mae's nearly awestruck.

Flora didn't know why Mrs Sherman, who never attended town events, had decided to come to the lighting of the tree but she thought perhaps she had been emboldened by the thought of a life without Mr Sherman. Flora took this as a very good sign.

Everyone admired the tree for a few minutes ("It will stay lit until New Year's Day," said Min), and then they began to drift away.

"Goodbye!" Flora and Olivia and Ruby called to Nikki.

Gigi and Olivia's grandfather walked to their car. Olivia had found her parents and her brothers and also Mr Pennington, who lived next door to her, and they made their way back to the Row Houses with Min, Ruby and Flora, turning left off Main Street on to Dodds Lane, then right on to Aiken Avenue. And there before Flora were the Row Houses, looking in the dark like a castle. They were actually eight attached houses that had been built in 1882, and they were the only ones of their kind in Camden Falls. Flora had already begun to think of the Row House residents, all twenty-five of them, as her very large family. She passed by first the Morrises' house, dark since the Morrises had gone away for Thanksgiving; then by the Willets' house, where Mr and Mrs Willet were probably eating supper; and then by the Malones' house, which was also dark, before turning on to their walk.

"See you tomorrow!" Flora called to Olivia as the Walters turned onto their own walk next door.

From down the dimly lit street she heard Mr Pennington and Robby Edwards and his parents and the Fongs calling goodbye and goodnight to one another. Ruby opened their front door and Min grabbed the mail from the letter box. She stood in the front hallway and leafed through the envelopes as Daisy Dear galumphed out of the kitchen and King Comma made a more subtle appearance.

"Huh," said Min, an open card in her hand. "This is from your aunt Allie, girls. She says she's planning to visit at Christmas and that she'll call soon to make arrangements. My stars. She hasn't visited Camden Falls in years."

This turned out to be bigger news than Flora could have imagined...

The story continues in...

'Tis the Season

Out in October 2012!

You'll also love...